March 1974

To Cathy – my
"bestest girl" –

Love,

Aunt Judy

THE DAHLBE FAMILY HORSE

Illustrated by Paul E. Kennedy

The Dahlbe Family Horse

by Laura Nelson Baker

THE DIAL PRESS   NEW YORK

Designed by Bernard Brussel-Smith
Printed in the United States of America
First edition

To those other children of Laurithz and Josie Nelson: my four brothers and five sisters, especially to my sister Myrtle, who gave me the idea, and my brother Adolph, for his help in remembering details accurately.

THE DAHLBE FAMILY HORSE

1. *chapter*

The Dahlbe family was eating breakfast at the round
oak table in the dining room because it was spring. In
the winter time, they ate the morning meal in the
kitchen, by the warm kitchen range, but Mama
Dahlbe, as soon as the weather warmed up enough,
was always in a hurry to get everyone into the pleasant
dining room for all the day's meals.

Hilmer, who was going on eight, was soaking thick
chunks of bread and butter in his cocoa, happily, but
Sarah, who was ten, ate her bread and butter like the
grownups and drank her cocoa separately. Her brother,

she thought with scorn, was still only a baby or he wouldn't eat in that greedy way.

"Your bangs need cutting again, Sarah," her mother said, studying her thoughtfully from across the table. "If there's anything that makes me nervous, it's seeing hair hang down in front of people's eyes. I don't want you to ruin your eyesight, the way mine was ruined." Mrs. Dahlbe pushed the metal-rimmed spectacles which rested halfway down her nose closer to her eyebrows.

"Hilmer's hair is always in his eyes," Sarah said. She liked to act grown-up, but she felt envious of her brother just the same. Bread soaked in cocoa that way was awfully good—the butter made shiny little circles on the cocoa, which gave the cocoa a good taste. She yearned to have just one piece before she left the table, but she wouldn't let herself.

"Well, Hilmer can't help it. His hair just grows that way." Mrs. Dahlbe removed the plate of butter in front of her son. "Now, that's enough butter. You've already spread it on an inch thick. Other people might like a little, too, you know."

Sarah's father, who had not been paying attention to the family conversation, suddenly looked up from his own breakfast of fried salt pork and potatoes, and said, "Our Birdie's not going to last another six months, unless I miss my guess."

There was silence around the table and it seemed to Sarah that even the hand-painted plates on the plate rail were stiffer than usual. Birdie was the Dahlbe family horse, the one that pulled the buggy in the summertime and the cutter in winter to take them all to church on Sunday, and to town to buy groceries during the week.

"Let's sell Birdie and get a pony." Hilmer had finished his cocoa and he set the empty cup down with a sigh. His eyes, which were the same light, bright blue as his father's, gleamed. "Mr. Rassmussen, out by Uncle Adolf's place, has a Shetland pony he wants to sell bad. I betcha we could get it awful cheap."

Sarah felt like hitting her brother. She didn't want a

3

Shetland pony. She didn't want any horse except Birdie. Why, Birdie was part of the family! Birdie had been born exactly ten years before Sarah, in March. They had almost the same birthday.

"Nobody would buy an old horse like Birdie, especially if she's as sick as Papa says," Mrs. Dahlbe said practically. She looked at Sarah. "Now, Sarah, don't you start to worry about it. Birdie's old and she's a little deaf, but we aren't going to get rid of her for a while yet. Wouldn't be any sense in it."

Sarah was comforted. She looked gratefully toward her mother, thinking how glad she was that Mama had brown eyes like her own and was round and cozy, not thin, like Sonora Holten's mother. Sarah was round, too, in a way, and she was not as glad about that as she was about her mother's roundness, but Mama said she would thin out as she grew taller.

Her mother looked back at Sarah, not exactly smiling, but with an expression that said more than her words had. Mama understood when she was feeling bad, Sarah thought, without being told. Sometimes Papa did, too, but not when it came to anything about the animals. Papa liked animals, but he said that farmers had to be sensible. Any farmer who kept sick or dying animals around the place, eating up hay and taking time that should go to other chores, was apt to

4

end in the poorhouse, and his family right along with him. Papa had been saying for a long time now that they couldn't really afford to keep Birdie much longer. She ate more hay than she was worth. The truth was, Sarah knew, that Papa wanted an automobile. He kept saying that the day of the horse was over and they ought to use Mama's chicken money to buy a Ford.

"You children hurry and finish now," Mama said to Hilmer and Sarah. "It's a quarter after eight. Papa's got Birdie all hitched up."

School began at nine. Hilmer and Sarah usually walked the mile and a quarter to the schoolhouse but today rain was coming down hard outside the windows, so Mr. Dahlbe was going to take them in. The Dahlbe children went to town school, in Cedar Grove, although they were really in the country school district. Papa had explained that because their front meadow was inside something called "the incorporation" that he didn't have to pay tuition money for Sarah and Hilmer in the town school. Sarah didn't understand what it was all about except that she didn't have to go to the little schoolhouse near Mill Creek, where the Knutson kids went. She was glad of it; the Mill Creek school had only one teacher for all the grades, and hardly any playground.

"You didn't leave our Birdie standing out in the rain all this time, Papa, did you?" Sarah asked. "She'll catch cold and get the heaves again."

Papa laughed and gave her a playful shove. "You don't know what the heaves are," he said. "And I should think you could trust me to look after the horse I drove when I courted your mother. Birdie's in the surrey barn, safe and dry—but she's going to have to be out in the rain all the way into town, you know."

Sarah guessed there wasn't any way to keep animals from getting wet when it was raining, if they had to be outdoors.

"Maybe Sarah could walk alongside the buggy and hold an umbrella over Birdie," Mama teased. "But hurry now, children."

"I'm all ready, except for my rubbers," Sarah said. "It's Hilmer who's always so slow." Because he's greedy and eats too much, she said to herself—but then, when her brother swallowed the last drop of his cocoa and marched over to the row of hooks by the kitchen door to put on his jacket and cap, she had to smile at him. His hair stuck up in cowlicks on the back of his head and in front, near the parting, and his stockings were always falling down or a button coming off his jacket. Still, Hilmer was usually chosen for recitations when there was a school program. It was partly because he learned pieces quickly, but

6

Mama said his big, wide smile helped, too. At Easter time last year, he had stood on the platform in the high-school assembly room, where all the classes were having a program, looking even smaller than he really was. Mama and Sarah, sitting together in the audience —Sarah's class had sung the opening song—had been scared to death that Hilmer would forget his piece. For almost a minute he didn't say a word, but then he smiled and began his recitation. Sarah looked around and saw that everybody else was smiling, too— smiling back at Hilmer.

"Don't forget your rubbers," she said to her brother, having pulled her own rubbers on by then. Papa had gone out to the surrey barn—the place under the hay-loft where the buggy and some farm machinery were kept in bad weather. There was no surrey there any more; it stood out in the woods now, falling to pieces, because Papa said it was no use fixing it up since it would be only a matter of time before they got an automobile.

"I don't need rubbers," Hilmer said breezily, but his mother turned around from the stove and caught him by the shoulder.

"Oh, yes, you do, young man. You sit right down and put those rubbers on. It rained all night. And you'll have to walk home after school, with the lane thick with mud."

7

"The rubbers come off in the mud," Hilmer grumbled, but his mother paid no attention. Hilmer gave in, but he glared at his sister.

"If you'd just kept your mouth shut for a change," he said to her when they were outdoors and running toward the buggy where their father was waiting for them, "Ma wouldn't have noticed about my rubbers."

"She would have noticed plenty when you got home tonight, with your shoes wrecked from the mud and the water," Sarah retorted.

She reached the buggy first and ran around in front of Birdie to get in on the other side. Papa was already in the driver's seat. She stopped to give the horse a soft pat on the side of her nose. Birdie whinnied softly, shaking her harness so that drops of water flew off to the sides of the buggy shafts. The rain was making her coat shine more than usual. Birdie was almost the same color as the chestnut Uncle Adolf had given Sarah. He had found the smooth, brown nut on the street in Mapleton. There weren't many chestnut trees in that part of Iowa, he said, but maybe somebody had a tree or two. He called it a horse chestnut because it was the same color as Birdie, Sarah decided.

"Don't stand out there in the rain, Sarah," Papa called to her. "No use my taking you to school if you're going to get soaked before you leave home."

8

Sarah clambered up onto the buggy step and her father pulled her in to sit beside him.

"Giddap there, Birdie," he said.

Hilmer always wanted to ride on the outside of the seat, even when, like today, the rain curtains were buckled on and there wasn't much he could see. Sarah liked to sit next to her father and watch the way he handled the reins, guiding Birdie without trying. Birdie was so used to Papa's touch on the reins, it was like a language between the two of them—a language that not even Mama understood, Sarah thought. Birdie was Papa's horse, even if he did keep saying they couldn't afford to keep her around any more.

Thinking about that, Sarah studied her father from her place beside him. Papa must have been even more handsome when he was Mama's beau. His hair was thick and dark and curly and he had a smile like Hilmer's. Even from under his mustache, when Papa smiled at her, the smile warmed Sarah from top to toe.

On the way into town, the Dahlbes stopped to pick up Sarah's friend Katie Rusley. Katie's mother was a widow and didn't have a horse and buggy. The day before, Katie had been home with a toothache. Her mother had taken her to the dentist, who had pulled out the aching tooth. Katie proudly showed Sarah the hole.

9

"The dentist said I was real brave," Katie boasted. She was thin and yellow-haired, with eyes that were between brown and green. She hardly ever sat entirely still. Now she started playing with the snap buttons on the buggy curtains.

"Papa gave me a dime once," Sarah told Katie, "for letting him pull out a loose tooth. I mean, he gave me the dime because I didn't cry, not even when it was bleeding all over me." She was not going to let her friend think she was the only brave person in the world.

Katie changed the subject. "I like rain," she said. She had on a new raincoat, with a hood. Sarah felt envious, for a minute, but then she remembered that Katie didn't have a Papa to take her to school in bad weather. It was better to have Papa than a new raincoat!

The buggy jolted suddenly as it hit a deep rut in the road and Papa jerked Birdie's reins. "Whoa, now, girl, whoa there," he said, "let's take it easy." Birdie got scared sometimes, when the buggy jerked and banged up against the backs of her legs.

There was a long hill leading up from the railroad station and the shining steel tracks, to the center of Cedar Grove. Birdie liked hills and she went up it at a nice, brisk pace. Sarah loved the clip-clop-clip sound Birdie's horseshoes made on the paving which covered the main street of town. Halfway up the hill they

10

passed the blacksmith's shop and could see the glow of the forge through the open doors.

"We're early for school so I'll have time to stop at the post office," Papa said. He kept a box in town instead of getting his mail rural free delivery like the farmers farther out in the country. When Papa didn't take them to school, Sarah stopped at the post office on her way home. On Saturdays, the whole family usually came in to Cedar Grove to bring cream to the creamery and eggs to the grocery store, exchanging the eggs for groceries. Any money left over was what Mama called her chicken money; she saved it for important things.

Papa handed Birdie's reins over to Hilmer and climbed out of the buggy. Old man Kornrud, who had come from Norway when he was too old to change his ways, was coming down the street. Nearly everybody in Cedar Grove had relatives in the "old country," which was what they called Norway, so nobody minded Mr. and Mrs. Kornrud's old-fashioned clothes or Norwegian talk.

As Papa came out of the post office he stopped to say something in Norwegian to Mr. Kornrud on the post office steps. Sarah's father was just going to get back into the buggy when Oscar Lund suddenly appeared and said, "Hold on there, Dahlbe, I want to tell you something."

Mr. Lund owned the brick garage at the end of Main Street, which sold Fords and gasoline and oil for tractors and cars.

"I saw some people over at Stantonville last week," Mr. Lund said when he got close enough to speak to Mr. Dahlbe. "They'll take that buggy horse of yours off your hands, if you decide to buy a Ford from me. You said last fall that you didn't want to give her up unless you knew somebody would find her useful."

Papa gave a brief glance toward where Sarah sat in the buggy, leaning forward. "Yah, well, I'll think about it when the time comes," he said. "It depends on how things go this year."

"You can have credit, Lars," Mr. Lund urged. "Lars Dahlbe's word is as good as a bank note. I wouldn't expect you to pay for the car all at once."

"Mr. Lund's rich," Katie whispered in Sarah's ear, but Sarah brushed her away, crossly. She didn't want to miss a word of what Papa said. Her heart had begun to pound a little, the minute Mr. Lund mentioned giving Birdie away. It was better than having her shot, the way people did with old horses sometimes, but not much better. Birdie wasn't just a horse, she was Sarah's best friend. Sarah glanced sidewise at Katie, hoping Katie wouldn't hear what was in her mind. Katie wouldn't like taking second place to a horse, not even Birdie.

Papa stood on the high curb of the sidewalk in the misting rain, his legs apart, looking across the street to where the Cedar Grove State Bank stood. Sarah didn't know if he was looking at the clock which jutted out from a corner of the bank or if he was thinking. She was relieved when he said, finally, "It's time I got these youngsters down to the school, Oscar. We'll talk about it some other time."

I hate Mr. Lund, Sarah thought, looking after the

prosperous garage owner. He was a director of the bank, Mama said—whatever a director was. He was even more important than the mayor, she guessed. But she hated him, anyway. Then, suddenly, she remembered what Pastor Lindgren had said when he talked to the Sunday school last week. He had said that to hate someone was the same as murder.

"Please, God," Sarah murmured quickly under her breath, "I didn't mean it. I don't really hate Mr. Lund—only I wish he wouldn't pester Papa about buying a Ford."

The rain had stopped by the time they reached the schoolhouse. Papa lifted Katie down first, and then Sarah—Hilmer didn't wait to be lifted; he jumped down, but Sarah loved to have her father put his strong hands under her arms and swing her wide of the buggy.

"Run in quick before it starts to rain again," he said to them.

"The first bell is ringing," Hilmer called back to the girls from the big doors of the building, where he was already grasping the iron handles.

"We're not deaf." Sarah walked around in front of the buggy, to say good-bye to Birdie. When she put her hand up to pat the horse, a drop of water ran down Birdie's nose, like a tear. Sarah knew it was rain water but it could just as well have been a tear, she told herself, after what Mr. Lund said to Papa. She would have to think of some way of saving Birdie from being given away. Papa would never get rid of his horse if Sarah could prove to him that Birdie earned her hay. That's what she would have to do: find some way of showing how valuable Birdie really was, in spite of her slowness and old age.

The next day was Saturday—no school! The sun was shining when Sarah woke and went down to breakfast, but Papa said that he couldn't work in the corn field after all, because the week of rain had left the ground too wet.

"I'll be out in the horse barn, if you want me for anything," he said to Sarah's mother when he had finished his meal. "Send Hilmer out as soon as he gets through stuffing himself." Mr. Dahlbe gave his son's cowlick a tug as he passed behind Hilmer's chair. "He can throw hay down for the horses, to earn his keep."

"Can I help, too, Papa?" Sarah begged. She loved going up into the haymow.

"Ask your ma about that. She needs help in the house, too, you know." Papa went outdoors without waiting to hear what Sarah's mother would say.

"First you wipe the dishes and make your and Hilmer's beds," Mama decided. "Then you can go out to the barn."

"I wish I was a boy." Sarah's lips started to form into a pout as her brother left the table, put on his cap and overall jacket, and headed for the barn. Then, catching her mother's frown, she decided she had better be careful. If she sulked, Mama might make her stay inside all morning.

"Hilmer wipes dishes, too, sometimes." Mrs. Dahlbe shaved slivers of soap off the white bar in her hand and stirred them around in the dish-pan of water which had been heating on the back of the stove. The kitchen sink was too small for the dish-pan, so the dishes were washed on top of the stove near the reservoir of warm water at one end of the range. Mama had a hot fire going because she was going to make cookies. "The water in the reservoir is good and hot now, for rinsing the dishes," she told Sarah. Sarah took a tin cup from the rinse-pan where her mother was putting the clean, soapy dishes, and lifting the lid of the reservoir, dipped

17

the cup into the clean, hot water and poured it over them.

Her mother said, "I don't think you'd be so anxious to be a boy when Easter time comes. Instead of a hat trimmed with flowers and ribbons, and new slippers, you'd maybe just get a new shirt or tie."

Easter was only two weeks away. Already Sarah's hat from last year had been dyed pink and had white daisies that Mama had bought from the milliner's store, and long streamers of new white ribbon. No, Sarah decided, she wouldn't want to be a boy at Easter time. Or Christmas. Maybe not even on Sundays.

"Katie's got a new blue organdy for Easter," Sarah said. The only organdy dress she owned was one that had been passed on from her cousin in North Dakota who was a year older than Sarah. It was white and when Mama starched the ruffles, it looked nice, but some day Sarah hoped to have a dress of colored organdy. Pink would be the best, especially the pale color of apple blossoms before they opened. Apple-blossom pink was Sarah's favorite color; Pastor Lindgren's wife had said to Mama once that Sarah's cheeks were the same color as apple blossoms.

Mrs. Dahlbe added more hot water to her dish-pan. "That's fine that Katie has a new dress. Her mother spends every cent she makes working for the printing office on that youngster, but I don't suppose you can blame a widow with only one child, and nothing else to live for, like Gert Rusley, poor woman. I was there the night they brought her husband home. He didn't live more than a few hours."

Sarah had heard the story many times of how Katie's father had been gored by a bull but she never grew tired of hearing it. Whenever she went down to Katie's to play, she looked at Mr. and Mrs. Rusley's wedding picture—and thought how terrible it must be to have a bull's horns stuck through your middle.

Her mother, however, didn't go on with the story, and Sarah tried to encourage her by saying, "Katie doesn't act spoiled, though, Mama. Not the way Mabel Linde does."

"Katie's a nice little girl," Mrs. Dahlbe answered absently. She glanced at the golden oak wall clock on the shelf in the dining room and saw its black hands pointing toward eight o'clock. "My, how the time flies. I have to get cookies baked and the bread done by four o'clock, because that's when Papa wants to go to town."

Seeing that her mother had completely forgotten about Mr. Rusley and the bull, Sarah concentrated on the dishes. Afterward, she went upstairs, to make first her own bed and then, going across the hall, she made her brother's bed. From Hilmer's room she looked out toward the barn. Papa was taking the work team out to the water tank to drink. At this time of the year there wasn't much hay left in the barn, and it was fun to play there.

Quickly, she pulled the cotton blankets on the bed straight—Hilmer slept so wildly that the covers were always every which way, making it hard to do the bed right. But if she didn't do a good job, Mama might come upstairs for something and see that she had been slapdash—the worst word her mother could think of, to describe anybody who did a poor job of work.

In the kitchen, as Sarah passed through on her way outdoors, the smell of cookies baking had already begun to fill the air. "Mmmm," she said, "sugar cookies!"

"Yah, it's Papa's turn to have what he likes best." Hilmer liked oatmeal cookies and Mama was fond of a new recipe she had gotten from Mrs. Rusley, that had peanut butter in it, but Papa and Sarah favored the thin, crisp cookies made of butter and cream and sprinkled on top with sugar. The sugar cooky recipe had come from Grandma Dahlbe.

"Shall I tell Papa to come in and have cookies and coffee?" Sarah asked.

"He can wait awhile. It's only an hour since breakfast. Anyway, there's only one pan out of the oven and they're still hot."

Sarah cast a hungry look at the cookies spread out

on wrapping paper at one end of the table, then went on her way.

The top half of the barn door was open but the bottom half was hooked on the inside, just below Sarah's reaching fingers.

"Climb over," Hilmer said.

Papa said, "Go let your sister in, Hilmer. Don't always be such a *torsk*."

Hilmer's face turned red. A *torsk* was a Norwegian fish that Papa didn't like. When he called either Sarah or Hilmer a *torsk*, it was the same as calling them "poor fish." Sarah gave Hilmer a triumphant look when he had to come and unhook the door for her, but he only ducked around her to beat her to the ladder leading to the haymow.

"I haven't thrown the hay down to the horses yet," he said. "Papa made me clean out Birdie's stall, first."

Cleaning out a horse stall was a nasty chore, and for once Sarah was glad she was a girl instead of a boy. Papa would never expect a girl to do work like that. She followed her brother up the haymow ladder and hauled herself onto the dusty-smelling floor of the upper barn. "When we've finished helping Papa feed the horses, let's play up here," she said to Hilmer.

"Then you've got to let me be king of the castle," said Hilmer.

Sarah glanced at the pile of hay remaining in the

north half of the barn. It was still big enough, maybe, to make a castle, but she didn't think it could be much fun to play king of the castle when there was only one person for him to keep off.

"You always want to be king of the castle," Sarah said. She went over to the mound of hay and began to gather up an armful. She and Hilmer had to carry the hay to the holes in the haybarn floor, above the horses' mangers, and push it through. There was a manger, or feed box, at the head of each one of the stalls.

Sarah dropped her first armload into Birdie's manger. If the sun kept shining and there wasn't too much mud in the barnyard, Papa might let her go for a ride on Birdie, after the horses were all cared for.

It didn't take Hilmer and Sarah very long to drop hay into all of the mangers. When Papa called up, "That's enough now," they were glad to quit, just the same. Sarah lay on her stomach at the edge of the hole where Papa was currying the team of grays, Frank and Maud. She liked to listen to the scraping sound the currycomb made when her father swept it in rhythmic downstrokes along the horses' flanks. It was almost as good as having her own back scratched—except she wouldn't want Papa to use a currycomb on her! Currycombs had wire teeth. Horses had tough skins, so currycombs felt good to them, Papa said.

"Can we play up here awhile?" Sarah asked her father.

"If you don't knock the hay all over the barn."

Sarah pulled herself upright and told Hilmer, "We can't play king of the castle because that will knock the hay pile down. You heard what Papa said. Besides, I want to talk to you about something important. Let's sit down on the hay a minute."

Hilmer eyed her cautiously but finally flopped down

23

beside her. "What do you want to talk about?" he wanted to know.

"About our Birdie." Sarah remembered that her brother had been perfectly willing to sell their old friend, if he could get a Shetland pony instead. After a minute's thought, she said, "You don't want Papa to get rid of Birdie, do you, even if he got you a pony? Papa thinks it costs too much to feed a big horse like Birdie, just for a pet. We'll have to prove, some way, that she's too useful to give away."

"She's useful now, but if we get a Ford, I don't see what good she'll be."

Sarah sighed. Hilmer wasn't going to be much use, she could see that. He didn't care about Birdie the way she did—not even as much as Mama and Papa did. He'd rather have an automobile, that was plain.

"Oh, go away and leave me alone," she said to him, scowling. "I want to think."

"I don't have to go anywhere because you say so," Hilmer retorted. However, he got up and went toward the ladder leading to the lower barn. "I'm hungry. I'm going into the house and find something to eat."

The cookies! Sarah had almost forgotten about them. She scrambled to her feet and ran after Hilmer.

𝕭 chapter

At noon, when the Dahlbe family was eating dinner, Sarah said, "Papa, can I ride Birdie out to the spring this afternoon?" She said the words breathlessly, uncertain what the answer would be.

"We're going to town about four o'clock." It was Sarah's mother who answered. "We don't want Birdie to get all tired out, first."

But Papa said, "A little run would do her good. Just don't stay out there in the back pasture dreaming, so somebody has to go looking for you, Sarah."

Sarah blushed and looked down at her plate. The last time she had ridden Birdie out to the west end of the farm, she had been so busy making up stories about when she would be grown up, that she had forgotten to come home for supper.

The noon dinner was potato dumplings in ham broth—Papa called the dumplings *komle* because that was what they were called in Norway. Sarah was not very fond of *komle* but she liked the piece of sausage Mama buried in the middle of each dumpling. She cut a dumpling open and took out the sausage. Then, glancing at her mother across the table, she realized that even though Mama seemed to be busy cutting meat off the ham bone, she had one eye on Sarah. Mama didn't like Sarah or Hilmer to be picky about food.

After everybody had eaten and Mama had allowed both Sarah and Hilmer two cookies each, Sarah waited, with as much patience as she could, for Papa and Mama to finish their coffee. At dinner time, no one could leave the table until Papa had thanked God for their food.

Finally, the thanks had been said and everyone got up from the table.

"Can I go and ride Birdie now, Mama?" Sarah asked.

Her mother pushed her empty chair up close under

the table. She stood leaning on it and looking down at Sarah for a minute. Mama's spectacles were sprinkled with flour and her hair, a lighter brown than Sarah's, had worked loose from the round knot on top of her head. Sarah, looking up into the soft eyes behind the flour-speckled eyeglasses, thought that Mama had the nicest, kindest face of anyone in the whole world.

"Oh, run along to your horse, since you think she's so wonderful," Mama said with a smile.

Sarah buried her nose in the crook of her mother's arm for a second—Mama smelled of cookies and warmth and sausage—and then went skipping out the back door toward the barn.

When she reached Birdie's stall, she saw that Papa had already put a bridle on the horse. "Come on," he said, "and I'll boost you onto her back. Don't forget to duck your head when you go through the door to the barnyard, though. You're big enough now to hit the frame. Where did Hilmer get to?"

"He said he was going out to the hog-house to look at the little pigs."

Her father frowned. "I hope he has sense enough to keep away from the sow. You remember what happened last year, when she had new pigs."

Sarah remembered. She and Hilmer had been picking up corn cobs to fill the cob basket Mama kept beside the kitchen range. They were supposed to get them from the lower part of the pigpen but there weren't as many there as there were closer to the hog-house.

"Let's go up closer," Hilmer had suggested, when their basket was only about half-full. "There are a lot of fresh cobs by the feeding trough."

Sarah looked up toward the trough. There weren't any pigs near it. They had just about filled the basket when Sarah heard a noise. Turning, she saw the mother sow charging out of the hog-house straight toward them!

"Run!" Sarah had yelled at her brother.

Both of them dropped the cob basket and made for the board fence as fast as they could. The sow was only a few feet behind them. Even after they had reached the safe side of the fence, they could hear her furious grunting.

"You've been told a thousand times," Mama had scolded Sarah, "to pick cobs in the other end of the pen."

"Hilmer's to blame. He said we should go up there," Sarah had protested.

But Mama had said, "You're the oldest, Sarah. You knew better. I don't want to hear any more of this trying to throw the blame on Hilmer."

You're the oldest. Sometimes it was nice to be the oldest but a lot of the time it was tiresome, Sarah

28

thought as she came out of the horse barn on Birdie's back and lifted her head. She pulled gently on the right rein of Birdie's bridle, to steer her toward the gate at the lower end of the barnyard. Because she was older than Hilmer, Mama sometimes told her things that Hilmer was too young to hear. This always made Sarah feel grown-up and proud. But then sometimes Mama would say that Sarah was older and should take responsibility for Hilmer. Sarah sighed, and clapping her heels lightly against Birdie's side, said, "Giddap, Birdie, let's go fast." Birdie didn't particularly like to gallop, but she would when Sarah urged her, once they were out of the barnyard and in the open pasture.

The smell of clover and alfalfa came across the meadow, from the hayfield across the railroad tracks. There was a slight breeze, and the rain had dumped enough water in the pond on the Dahlbe side of the tracks to nearly cover the tent-shaped muskrat houses made of sticks and weeds and mud. The breeze rippled the pond water, making it glitter in the sunshine. Sarah put her head down for a minute against Birdie's neck, liking the scratchy feeling of horsehair against her face, but liking even more the horsy smell that mingled with the smell of the hay.

She urged Birdie toward the fence which separated the Dahlbe farm from its neighbor farm on the west, threw the reins over a fence post, and slid off the horse.

29

Crawling under the fence, Sarah made her way to a pile of rocks at the corner of the farm where their fence met the neighbor's.

On one side of the pile she had built up a kind of cupboard to protect some treasures she had collected from frost or water. The cupboard was made of flat stones arranged to leave a cave in the middle. Reaching in the cave, Sarah pulled out a little jar of salve the postmaster had given her. He said it was a free sample that had come in the mail. She unscrewed the lid of the jar and smelled it. There wasn't much smell, but it was a pretty, pale yellow color, and very smooth. She put the lid of the jar back on. There were several marbles which had been given to her by Sonny Lund. She didn't play marbles, but they were pretty, and if she left them around the house, Hilmer would borrow them. One by one she took out the other items: the small, pink drinking glass with bubbles in it that she had found in the ditch by the highway—it had a small crack but was lovely—and an old calendar picture of a white boat on blue water with an orange moon hanging in the sky. Sarah had never been on a boat but she loved the picture.

The shiny chestnut Uncle Adolf had given her was there and the butterfly cocoon Hilmer had found under the front porch. Sarah saw that the cocoon had shriveled up; it would never be a butterfly, now. Looking at it made her sad and she threw the remains away.

Everything else went back into the cupboard and then Sarah climbed to the top of the biggest rock on the pile. She needed to put her mind to the problem of Birdie. First, she would try to convince Papa that Birdie was valuable. "Remember how she pulled Mama all over the township in the buggy, when Mama was delivering catalogs?" Sarah planned to say to Papa.

The trouble was that it had been three years since Mama had taken on the job of delivering mail-order catalogs to the farmers, and Birdie hadn't been quite as old then.

Sarah concentrated harder. But what about the time when Hilmer was four and had fallen down and cut himself on the foot scraper outside the back door? Papa was in the fields when it happened, and Mama had sent Sarah to call him home. But when they got back to the house, Mama had already harnessed Birdie to the buggy and gone to the doctor's, leaving a note for Papa.

Hilmer had four stitches taken in his cheek that day; he still had a scar from it. The doctor had said that if Mama hadn't come to him right away, Hilmer could have bled to death. If Mama hadn't had Birdie, she couldn't have taken Hilmer in so quickly, could she?

Sarah hopped down off the rock. Her father had probably forgotten all about how Birdie had saved Hilmer's life. Sarah made her way back to the fence and lifted the bridle reins off the fence post. Climbing to the top strand of the barbed wire, and clinging to the wooden post, she coaxed Birdie near enough so that she could jump onto the horse's back.

"Papa will never give you away, our Birdie," she said confidently as they started home. "I promise."

4 *chapter*

It was a whole week before Sarah found a chance to talk to her father about Birdie and remind him of how Birdie had saved Hilmer's life. It was Saturday again and Papa had asked her to come and turn the wheel on the grindstone while he sharpened his axe and some of his other tools. The sun had been shining nearly every day all week and as soon as Papa finished at the grindstone, and chopped some wood, he was going out into the fields.

"If there's anything worse than a blunt axe, I don't

34

know what it is," Papa said to Sarah, feeling the edge of his blade with a cautious thumb.

Sarah, resting while he checked the axe, thought how little she liked helping Papa at the grindstone. She didn't like the sound the axe blade made when Papa held it against the stone wheel, and she didn't like to stand in the mud the water made when Papa poured it over the turning stone. Turning the handle that worked the wheel made her arms ache, too. Usually, Hilmer was the one who turned the grindstone, but Hilmer was sick in bed.

"You'll have to go into town alone tonight, with the eggs," Sarah's mother had said to Papa that morning, when she found out Hilmer's forehead was hot. "I asked Pastor Lindgren and his wife out for Sunday dinner, so you'd better buy some butter at the store; my churning wasn't good this week."

"Better not ask folks to come where there's sickness," Papa had said, but Mama had answered it was too early to tell if Hilmer was sick with something that was catchy or not. Sarah, knowing her brother had sneaked a big handful of prunes the night before, was pretty sure that Hilmer would be all right by tomorrow, but she said nothing.

"Keep turning that handle," Papa said, frowning at Sarah.

She had been so busy daydreaming, she had stopped

working the grindstone. There was her father, holding the axe and the tin pitcher of water to pour over the wheel, but the wheel wasn't moving! Sarah looked at Papa sheepishly.

Then, suddenly, a pheasant rose out of the grass in the orchard, near where the grindstone was set, and both Sarah and her father turned their heads to watch the bird.

"They'll be nesting soon now," Papa said. "They get a lot of our corn in the fall, but I can't help liking them just the same. A pheasant's about the prettiest bird you could hope to see anywhere."

He lifted the axe blade off the stone and tested it once more. "I guess it's sharp enough," he said to Sarah. "You can go now."

"Papa. . . ." Sarah watched the water drip off the grindstone wheel onto the ground, trying to think how to begin about Birdie and Hilmer.

At last, Papa smiled at her. "I suppose you think you should go to town with me tonight, is that it?"

"Yes, but that wasn't what I was going to say. I was thinking about Birdie—"

"You're always thinking about Birdie!"

"Well, remember, when Hilmer was only four years old, and he fell against the foot scraper?"

"Sure I remember. He's still got a scar—Doc says

36

he'll have it all his life, but I don't know. Anyway, it don't amount to much." Mr. Dahlbe put his axe up over his shoulder and began to walk toward a pile of wood at the edge of the orchard. Sarah tagged after him.

"No, but if it hadn't been for our Birdie, Hilmer might have died. I mean, if Birdie hadn't been here for Mama to hitch up to the buggy and get Hilmer into the doctor's so fast, he might have bled to death."

"Well, now, I don't think that's so." Her father lifted some wood from the top of the pile, setting it aside to pull out drier wood from below. "Stand back, girl. I don't want you to get in the way of my axe. Or of any flying chips, either. I have to work fast, your mother's almost out of fuel for the cook stove."

"Papa, he would too have bled to death! Mama said so. Except for Birdie's getting him to the doctor quick."

Her father concentrated his attention on wood-splitting for a few minutes. Then he stopped, resting the axe handle against the woodpile, to wipe the sweat from his face. "I'll tell you something, little Sarah," he said. "Your ma's a great one to imagine the worst. Hilmer was in no danger of bleeding to death, except in your ma's imagination—but I'm glad she took him into town right away, anyway." He lifted another

chunk of wood from the pile and picked up his axe
again. "If we'd had a Ford," he said, "she would have
got him there even faster."

Sarah gasped. "Mama wouldn't ever drive an automobile! She'd be scared to death."

Down came the axe, right in the middle of the
chunk of wood.

"I'm not so sure about that," said Papa.

Sarah stood watching her father a few minutes.

Then she asked, "Can we afford a car, Papa?" hoping that the answer would be no.

"That depends—we could buy on credit the way other folks do."

Sarah stared at him. She had heard her parents say many times over that they didn't believe in buying anything until they had the money saved to pay for it. She was so upset by what Papa had said that she turned and started for the house. Her father had to call after her to come and get a load of split kindling for the woodbox, the way she had been told to.

Sarah found Hilmer sitting up at the table when she went into the house. He looked better. His eyes were bright instead of the lifeless color they had been when he got up that morning.

"Hilmer wants breakfast," Mama said, "but I don't think he should put any food into his stomach just yet, do you, Sarah?"

Sometimes Mama just wanted another person to tell her to do what she planned to do anyway. If Hilmer was terribly hungry, he could get sick all over again from having an empty stomach. Hilmer gave his sister a pleading look. She hesitated.

"Why don't you fix him some milk toast, Mama?" she asked. She and Hilmer often had milk toast when they didn't feel well.

"Of course! Maybe you could put some bread in the oven. And put some extra in for yourself. You didn't eat much breakfast."

The milk toast tasted wonderful to Sarah, after working with her father outdoors. When she had finished her bowlful, she went back to the wood pile and brought in several armfuls of kindling wood. By the time she was through with that and the other Saturday chores, it was dinner time.

"We'll eat late today," her mother said, "because Papa doesn't want to come in from the field until it's near time for town. Did he say you could go with him, Sarah?"

Sarah looked around from where she was dusting the bay window in the sitting room and said in a surprised voice, "How did you know?"

Her mother laughed. "I put the idea in his head. Papa never likes to go to town on Saturday by himself and I have to stay home with Hilmer. Sarah, give the plants some water when you put them back in the window. I meant to water them yesterday but I didn't get around to it."

There were two geraniums and one other plant which had thick, shiny leaves, in the wide bay window. Sarah's mother liked to watch things grow. Whenever the family went for a ride in the country behind Birdie, or with Uncle Adolf in his Ford, Mrs. Dahlbe studied the fields on both sides of the road, and the clumps of trees beside some of the fences, telling Papa what he could see for himself: that the trees were leafing out, or that the corn in the Thompsons' field was up two inches, or that the wild plum trees had spread along the fences halfway to town.

At the edge of Holler's Woods, on the way to town, a wild crab-apple tree bloomed every spring, much earlier than the apple trees in the orchard. Every morning, when Sarah passed the woods on her way to school, she looked to see if the crab tree had turned pink yet, so she could tell her mother. Mama and Sarah agreed that it was almost summer, when the crab-apple tree bloomed. There were wildflowers in Holler's Woods, too—jack-in-the-pulpit, wake robins, and May apples. May apples were the most exciting to Sarah, because you had to look underneath the big umbrella leaves to see if there was a blossom or not.

It was late afternoon before Mr. Dahlbe had come in from his field work, eaten dinner, fed the pigs and milked the four cows in the cow barn.

"I'm going to teach Sarah to milk cows pretty soon," he said as he brought in a pail of milk to let settle so Mama could skim cream from it. Most of the cream was taken to the creamery to be made into butter, but the Dahlbes kept some for their own use. "Sarah's getting to be a big girl, now."

"I'm not going to milk that big Holstein, ever!" Sarah said in alarm. When she and Hilmer went to the lower pasture to chase the cows home for Papa to milk at night, the big Holstein bellowed like a bull and wouldn't go along with the other cows at all.

"How's the boy?" Papa asked Mama after he had set the milk pail on the kitchen table. He looked into the sitting room where Hilmer was propped up with pillows on the leather-covered couch. Mama had given Hilmer her old scissors and the sample book of wallpaper from the mail-order company to cut pictures from, but Sarah could see that her brother didn't take much interest in what he was doing. Hilmer hated being in bed, even when he had the measles, and if it was only the prunes that had made him sick, he was probably feeling lots better by now.

"Come on in here and see me, Papa," Hilmer called.

"I have to get these muddy shoes off first." Mr. Dahlbe sat down on a chair near the back door and removed his heavy, mud-laden shoes.

"He's lots better." Mrs. Dahlbe handed her husband a newspaper to set his dirty shoes on. She had just finished scrubbing the floor an hour earlier. "But if we took him to town, he'd go chasing off with the other boys and probably be sick all over again."

"No, I wouldn't," Hilmer called from the sitting room. "I'd keep quiet—just maybe walk around a little. Honest, Mama, I'd be careful."

"Yah, I know how careful you'd be." It was clear from Mrs. Dahlbe's tone of voice that she was not going to change her mind. Mama and Hilmer would stay home and let Papa and Sarah go in to town alone.

Mr. Dahlbe walked through the clean kitchen and dining room to the sitting room in his stockinged feet. He sat down beside Hilmer and looked him over. "What did you put into yourself this time?" he asked Hilmer. "Last time you were sick it was baked beans but we haven't had beans lately."

Hilmer grinned and looked down at his lap. He glanced sideways at Sarah as if he wanted her to tell about the prunes but she didn't. He could tell or not tell himself, she thought. His father rumpled his hair and then went to sit in the big, black rocker to rest before preparing to go to town.

Sarah went into the kitchen where her mother was filling the biggest wash basin with warm water from the reservoir. "You'll have to have your bath now," Mama said, "if you're going to be ready in time. Papa will want to wash up as soon as he's rested, so you want to be through by then." She shut the door between the sitting room and the dining room. "I didn't want to get out the washtub—you had a tub bath last week so I think you can scrub well enough with the basin, this week." She set the basin on one of the kitchen chairs, spreading newspaper on the floor around it, and told Sarah to get undressed.

"Can I wear my blue dress?" Sarah asked. The blue dress had been new at Christmas and she usually only wore it to Sunday school and church, but it would soon be summer and sateen would be too warm and wintry for the coming months.

Her mother thought for a minute. "Oh, I guess so. The brown dress has a rip in the sleeve and I don't have time to mend it before you go. But be careful getting in and out of the buggy. I don't want axle grease on that material. You're going to need it for school next year, after we make you another winter dress to wear for good."

As Sarah scrubbed, she listened to the sound of the teakettle on the range, the crackle of the fire in the firebox of the stove, giggles from Hilmer in the sitting room and Papa's big laugh, and her mother's soft humming as she stirred something in a pan on the stove.

"Mama," Sarah asked when she had finished washing and was putting on the clean underwear her mother had laid across a chair back, "do horses take baths?"

Her mother burst into a laugh, turning from the stove to look at Sarah. "Now, that's something I never heard anyone ask before in my life! It would take you, you little question box, to think of it. No, horses don't take baths—not with water, anyway. It's something like a bath when Papa cleans them with the curry-comb."

"And of course they get rained on." Sarah pulled on her long black stockings and fastened them to the garters dangling from her underwaist. "Anyway, Birdie is clean. She must be, because she always smells good."

"Oh, you and your Birdie!" Mama said.

Papa yelled from the other room to ask if Sarah was so dirty she had to take all day to get herself clean. Sarah stopped dawdling and put her petticoat over her head, then her blue dress, and pulled them down around herself.

"I'm all through!" she called out, going to the closed door and throwing it open. Mama would have to re-braid her hair, but they didn't need the kitchen for that. Sarah began to feel more and more excited about the trip into town. She had never gone in alone with Papa before. Feeling sorry for her brother, she went into the sitting room and sat down on the big couch beside him. "Do you want me to play cat and rat with you, Hilmer?" she asked. "I don't have anything to do until Mama calls me to fix my hair."

Hilmer sat up eagerly and Sarah went to the desk in the corner to see if there was a scrap of paper they could use to make the squares on. She found a half-sheet of an old school tablet and a stub of a pencil. Taking them back to the couch, she decided, feeling very pleased with herself, that she would let Hilmer win for once.

5 *chapter*

There was still a little light left on the hills and fields when Birdie pulled the buggy out of the last mudhole in the lane and emerged onto the highway leading to town. The light wasn't strong enough to give the trees and telephone poles a shadow, but there was enough for Sarah to see that the Larsons' bull was standing near the roadside fence, with only a wooden gate between him and the road. Her father saw the bull, too, and knowing how frightened of him Sarah was, he looked down at her and said, "The gentleman is safe

47

behind Knut Larson's gate, so don't look so worried, girl." Papa always referred to bulls as "gentlemen" cows, when he was talking to girls or ladies, but Sarah didn't think the bull that had killed Katie's father could have been much of a gentleman.

Despite her father's reassurances, Sarah moved a little closer to him as Birdie trotted past the bull. Papa put the reins in his left hand and put his right arm around her shoulders. Sarah relaxed against him, feeling warm and safe. When they reached the top of the hill, on Main Street, he said, "We'll take the big egg crate around to the poultry house and tie Birdie up there, Sarah." Mama didn't need many groceries and Papa was going to sell the eggs at the poultry house, instead of trading them at the store.

The poultry house was on a side street. They drove down as far as the barbershop and turned left. Two of Sarah's schoolmates were waiting to cross the street and she leaned out of the buggy to call to them as Papa clucked to Birdie to speed up and get out of the children's way.

One of the girls said, "It's Sarah Dahlbe," and waved after the buggy.

"Papa, after we get rid of the eggs, can I go and walk with Sonora and Alice?" Sarah asked, looking wistfully down the street after her friends.

48

"Mama doesn't approve of girls chasing around town on Saturday nights," Papa said. This was not quite the same as his saying no, Sarah decided, so she kept still.

The owner of the poultry house was just going to lock his door when he saw Mr. Dahlbe and waited. "Eggs have been coming in so slow that I figured nobody would bring me any more tonight," he said.

"The Missis has some good layers," Papa said. He set the double crate on the poultry house counter. "She never spares herself, when it comes to raising chickens. I tell her she thinks more about them than she does about me and the kids."

Sarah wandered impatiently toward the door. She didn't want her father to stand there talking so long that her girl friends would think she had gone back home.

At last Papa took Sarah's hand in his and they went toward Main Street. At the barbershop corner, Sarah looked down the street for Sonora and Alice, but didn't see them.

Uncle Adolf was coming out of the barbershop, though. Sarah wrinkled her nose at her uncle. "You smell good," she told him. Uncle Adolf wasn't married but he had his own farm. And a tractor and an automobile. Mama said Uncle Adolf was the best catch in the county. He leaned over now and held his face against Sarah's for a second. "Take another smell," he said. "It won't cost you a *cent*."

Sarah laughed at his joke and sniffed. Uncle Adolf had a mustache, like Papa, except that her uncle's was smaller and darker and he kept it very neatly trimmed. His hair was darker than Papa's too, but his eyes were the same blue as Papa's and Hilmer's.

Uncle Adolf gave Sarah's braids a small tug, and reaching into his pocket, brought out a dime. "Here, buy a treat for yourself," he said.

A dime! Sarah's fingers closed around the treasure. Papa usually gave her a couple of pennies to spend when they came to town, but it wasn't often she had a whole dime just for nothing.

"What do you say, Sarah?" Papa prompted her.

"*Mange tak*, Uncle Adolf." Sarah said her thanks in Norwegian, to please her uncle.

"Papa, can I go across the street and spend the dime now?" Sarah asked. She was pretty sure she would find her school friends either in the Grove Grocery, or Nielsons' General, or the drug store.

"Yah, yah, run along." Papa's voice was impatient. "But see that you are in the grocery store in half an hour. I don't want to go hunting all over town for you when it's time for home."

50

Sarah promised and went skipping off quickly before he could change his mind and say she had to stay with him.

She found Sonora and Alice in the drug store. They were drinking a cherry-ade and Sarah considered whether or not she should spend a nickel for a glass of the bright red drink. She decided not to. The last cherry-ade she had, at the church picnic, had made her sick.

The owner of the drug store said, "You can sit on a stool while you wait, if you want to. We're not busy yet."

Sarah thanked him and hoisted herself up, letting her legs dangle; they weren't long enough to reach the floor from such tall stools. The drug store was one of her favorite places in town. It smelled of medicine but it had other smells, too: ice cream, fruit juices, chocolate, butterscotch, and perfume. In summer time, the drug store was the coolest place in town.

The girls finished their drinks and all three, Sonora, Alice, and Sarah, went outside to stroll up one side of Main Street and down the other.

"There's going to be a baptism in church tomorrow," Sonora said as they were walking along. "It's my cousin Rose's baby, that's how I know."

"I love to watch babies being baptized," Sarah said and the others agreed. Sonora thought the baby was to be called Martin George but she wasn't sure. There were three churches in Cedar Grove but most of Sarah's friends belonged to the Lutheran Church, which was the biggest.

The three friends parted company when the clock on the outside of the bank said eight-fifteen. Sonora and Alice said they had to go home and Sarah had to meet Papa.

Her father was not in the grocery store yet. She was glad because she had decided to spend her dime for candy and it took a long time to choose. She stood in front of the glass candy case and looked first at the butterscotch wafers and corn kernel candy, and then at the chocolate stars. The chocolate stars cost the most, which meant she wouldn't get many for a dime, but they were her favorite.

The clerk behind the counter asked, "Do you want something, Sarah?"

"I'm just thinking," Sarah said.

"I'll wait on somebody else, then, first."

In the penny candy box on the counter, there were little white bottles of wax candy. The bottles had red juice in them, that you could drink, and afterward you could chew the wax. The wax didn't have much taste but Hilmer liked the little bottles. Maybe she would get a nickel's worth of penny candies, like the wax bottles and licorice sticks, and then a nickel's worth of

chocolate stars. She began to pick out five penny items from the box.

"I see you're here," Papa said from behind her as she arranged her choices on the candy counter.

Sarah turned around and looked up at him. "I'm spending my dime," she explained. "Are you ready to go now?"

He shook his head. "I have to get a few things for your ma. Take your time." He added another nickel to Sarah's dime, which she had laid on the counter. "Buy a nickel's worth of peppermint drops, while you're at it."

Mr. Dahlbe and Sarah were ready to go out the door with their purchases when who should come into the store but Katie and Mrs. Rusley!

"Did you walk to town?" Sarah asked, astonished.

"We got a ride." Katie was so interested in what Sarah had bought that she didn't bother to explain further, but Mrs. Rusley, her face faintly pink, said to Mr. Dahlbe, "Andrew Sorenson called up to ask if he could come by and take us into town."

"Andy Sorenson, huh?" Papa fingered his mustache a second. "Well, Sorenson's a fine man. I've never understood how some woman hasn't happened to get hold of him. I guess he's a born bachelor, like my brother."

"Yah, well, I guess so . . ." Mrs. Rusley said vaguely. She moved on past Sarah and her father, into the store.

Sarah barely had time to tell Katie about the baptism in church the next day, before her father was urging her ahead of him out to the sidewalk. "It's almost nine o'clock," Papa said. Taking Sarah by the hand, Papa hurried her along toward Birdie and the buggy, a bag of groceries in his other hand. The stars were out now and the night sky was a purple-blue. If she could stay awake on the ride home, Sarah thought happily with a yawn, she would see how many stars she could count.

54

The last day of school was sad, Sarah thought, as she and Katie left the building and started out along the road leading to their homes. She had cleaned out her desk the day before and had taken home most of her books, pen and pen points, color crayons, and what was left of her tablet, leaving only a sheet of paper and a pencil in case she needed them the last day. Yesterday, Papa had driven Birdie and the buggy in, to get her and Hilmer and their school things. Hilmer's class had been let out for the summer yesterday, but hers and Katie's, the fourth grade, had a half-day session today to receive their report cards.

"I think Miss Steenson was mean to give me a C in geography," Katie said as the two girls passed the marsh that lay between town and Katie's home. Nobody used the marsh except about a million blackbirds and ten million mosquitoes and when the weather was warm at night, hundreds of fireflies. Probably plenty of snakes, too, Sarah thought; she had never set foot in the marsh so she didn't know. A red-winged blackbird flew toward a cattail reed, and perching on it, sang his long, chirring song. The reed swayed back and forth so hard Sarah was sure the blackbird would fall off, but he didn't.

"Hilmer got a C in deportment," Sarah said. She didn't want to talk about their teacher, Miss Steenson, because she liked her even if Katie didn't.

"Your mother's going to have a fit about Hilmer's bad mark in deportment, isn't she?" Katie picked up a stick and began to stir water that had collected in a rut at the side of the road. It had rained hard again the night before—it had rained so much lately that Mama was afraid her strawberries wouldn't ripen as they should.

"Come on!" Sarah said impatiently. "If you don't hurry, I won't have time to stop at your house. Mama expects me home by half past three."

Katie dropped the stick and they went on again. The Rusley house was visible now between the box elder trees that shaded it from summer sun. "Mama's baking bread today," she told Sarah. "If it's out of the oven, she'll let us have a piece, with butter and sugar."

"Mmmmm . . ." Sarah sighed in anticipation. Her own mother disapproved of her having bread warm from the oven. Mama said eating hot bread was a good way to get stomach ache. But Katie's mother laughed at that idea. Who could get sick from bread, she asked, when it was the staff of life?

It was cool and pleasant on the Rusleys' back step where Sarah and Katie sat to eat their bread and butter and sugar. The leaves of the box elders made patterns like black lace on the narrow sidewalk leading from the Rusleys' back door to the pump and the water tank.

"Your mother makes wonderful bread," Sarah said to Katie, lingering over the last few bites of her slice. Mama said Mrs. Rusley was the best bread baker around—and usually added that, on the other hand, there wasn't a soul to hold a candle to herself, when it came to making pie.

"I guess I'd better start home," Sarah said when she had swallowed the last crumb of bread and had licked the butter and sugar from her fingers. She stood up and went into the house to thank Katie's mother. She was not in the kitchen, so Sarah went into the dining room. She was not anywhere in the downstairs rooms, and Sarah was going to call up the stairs to her when she saw the vacant place on the wall where the Rusleys' wedding picture had always hung. She said to Katie, who had followed her inside, "What happened to your picture?"

"I dunno. Mama took it down." Katie didn't seem to be bothered by the picture's absence, but it gave Sarah a queer feeling to have it gone.

Mrs. Rusley called down to them, asking what they wanted.

"I'm going home," Sarah called back. "Thanks for the good bread."

By the time she had walked through her own lane and was climbing the knoll on which their house sat, Sarah was warm again. Grasshoppers were thick now in the lane, and because of the rain, the grass had grown high on both sides of the narrow road, even between the ruts. Sarah didn't like grasshoppers. They moved so suddenly they could jump on you when you weren't expecting it. The Dahlbes' garden was on the flattest part of the knoll, where the lane turned to the right and led around their house to the side yard. Mama was working in the strawberry patch when Sarah got there. Seeing Sarah, her mother called out, "Well, did you pass into fifth grade?"

"Oh, Mama!" Sarah said, half-laughing, half-angry. She walked closer to her mother.

Mama rested her hoe and looked at Sarah. "It could happen. I'm not the teacher. I don't know how dumb or smart you are."

"I got four A's and one B," Sarah said proudly. The B was in drawing. She never got higher than a B in that. Mama said none of the Dahlbes or the Torgesons were artistic.

Mama came to the fence, and leaning her hoe against it, put her hands on the wire mesh. "Did anybody else get higher marks than you?" she asked.

"No—but Sonora got the same, except her B was in arithmetic."

Mama said she didn't think children should work for grades—they should study hard in order to learn—but she always wanted to know where Sarah stood in her room, just the same.

"I'm glad you do your school work well, Sarah," Mama said. She thought education was the most wonderful thing in the world and she was trying to save some money in order for Sarah and Hilmer to go both to high school and college. Papa said he didn't see any sense in a girl going to college, since girls just got married, anyway. Mama always answered, "I want her to go to normal school and be a teacher, even if she gets married later. I always wanted to be a teacher."

Sarah, looking up over the fence into her mother's proud eyes, felt suddenly overwhelmed with love. "Mama . . ." she began. She wanted to say something like "Mama, I love you," except that nobody in their family ever said things like that.

"What?" her mother asked, brushing wisps of hair back from her sun-pinked cheeks. Mama's skin was fair and thin, and an hour outdoors turned her face pink.

Sarah, clutching her report card and the sweater she had taken off coming up the lane, said, "Katie's mother has taken down the picture of her and Mr. Rusley when they got married." It wasn't at all what she had wanted to say, but it would hold her mother's attention for a minute.

Mrs. Dahlbe's forehead puckered a little. She said, "Yah, well I guess she's one that's bound to have a man. And Sorenson is a good one."

"Do you mean that Mrs. Rusley's going to get married?" Sarah asked with interest. If Mrs. Rusley got married again, Katie would have a stepfather.

Mama picked up her hoe again. "Go on in and change into overalls. I want you to help me pick berries. A lot of them are almost ripe—they'll finish ripening in the house. I've been calling around to different places to see who wants strawberries, and tomorrow we'll hitch up Birdie and make deliveries. Papa's going to put Hilmer to work pulling mustard out of the corn fields tomorrow."

Sarah didn't especially like to pick strawberries, but she did like to go riding with her mother in the buggy, so she hurried on to the house without any fuss. Delivering strawberries was fun, but pulling mustard weeds wasn't. She would probably have to pull weeds, too, now that school was out, but at least she didn't have to start tomorrow.

There was no one in the house when Sarah went in. A cake was cooling on the table and the kettle of milk Mama was souring for making cottage cheese was on the back of the range. The back door was open—Papa had put the screen on the week before—and the air coming in smelled of summer. Now the last day of school didn't seem sad, Sarah thought, climbing the back stairs to her bedroom. She hoped it wouldn't rain tomorrow so they would be able to go out with the buggy. She hadn't ridden Birdie in a long time because Birdie hadn't been looking well, Papa said. Just the night before, after he'd taken Birdie to bring Sarah and Hilmer home from school, he had said to Mama, "She's not right, that horse. There's something ailing her."

Mama had given him a sharp look and answered,

"There's something ailing you, you mean. And I know what it is. Engine fever, that's what you've got, Lars Dahlbe."

Sarah, remembering that conversation, frowned as she slipped off her skirt and unbuttoned her blouse. What if it should be a good year for Papa's crops and he would have the money to pay for a Ford in the fall, without even using Mama's chicken money! She didn't even like to think about it.

The sun was bright in a blue, washed sky when Sarah opened her eyes the next morning. She woke up early without being called, remembering it was the first day of summer vacation and that she and Mama were going riding along the country roads, behind Birdie. She jumped out of bed and dressed quickly, wanting to have the fun of surprising her mother and father by getting up before she was called. She discovered, when she got downstairs, that no one was in the kitchen and the stove was cold. It was a funny feeling to be the first one up, and for a moment she thought maybe she would go back upstairs and lie down again. But then she saw her father coming from the barn with the milk and realized that he was up but hadn't started a fire in the stove because it was such a warm morning. Mama would cook breakfast on the kerosene stove under the windows.

"Go *dag*, early bird," Mr. Dahlbe greeted Sarah in Norwegian.

"Is Mama still sleeping?" Sarah watched as her father set down his milk pail and lit the kerosene stove.

"Sleeping!" Papa was scornful. "Not that ma of yours. She's out in the chicken house, looking after her baby chicks."

Sarah was mildly disappointed at not being able to claim that she was the first one up, but it was nicer to have company. "I'll set the table, Papa, and surprise Mama when she comes in from the chicken house," she said. "I'm going to help her all morning, so we can start out early with the strawberry boxes."

In spite of Sarah's help, however, it was almost two o'clock in the afternoon before Birdie was hitched to the buggy and they were ready to go. The boxes of strawberries which Mama had been keeping fresh in the cool cellar were loaded into the back part of the buggy, and Sarah and her mother sat in the front seat. Papa and Hilmer went out to the granary to shell corn before going back out to the fields; the house was left to look after itself for a few hours.

Sarah said that the house looked lonesome with no one in it.

"Just so it doesn't run away," Mama said, clicking to Birdie to get her started.

63

Mama didn't drive fast but let Birdie find her own pace as they clop-clopped along the country roads.

"It's a rest for me, riding in the buggy," Mama said. "Keeps me off my feet. I get pretty tired these days, but I guess it's only natural."

Sarah, who had been watching a brown wren skitter across the road in front of Birdie, looked at her mother in surprise. "Why, Mama? Are you sick?" Her mother was hardly ever sick but once she had had the grippe and been in bed a whole week.

With the hand not occupied in holding Birdie's reins, Mrs. Dahlbe lifted her daughter's braids back from her neck and let them drop against Sarah's shoulders. She looked down at Sarah, and then off over the green meadows and the black, plowed fields with their rows of young corn, their pale shoots of oats and barley.

"No, I'm not sick," she said. "I think you're big enough now to know about things ahead of time, maybe. In the fall, you and Hilmer are going to have a baby brother or sister. When a woman is going to have a baby, she gets tired more easily. That's what I meant."

"I hope it's a girl!" Sarah was thrilled at being told the news. The Larsons down the road had a new baby almost every year, but Mama had said that God hadn't seen fit to send any to the Dahlbes, since Hilmer. Now it looked as if God had finally seen fit.

Mama slapped the reins against Birdie's neck, to urge her away from some water that had collected at the side of the road. "You'll be allowed a drink when we get to the next farm," she told the horse. To Sarah she said, "You'll have an argument with Papa about having a girl. He wants another boy. I don't care, girl or boy, and Hilmer hasn't been asked what he wants."

They rode along in silence awhile, each of them thinking more than talking. Sarah was trying to imagine what it would be like to have a baby in the house again—Hilmer had been a baby once and she could remember a little about that, but not much. She didn't know what her mother was thinking, but whatever it was, it must be pleasant because Mama's face was very happy-looking.

By five o'clock all but a few boxes of the strawberries had been sold. Not all of the farmers bothered with raising strawberries and some that did had had bad luck because of the rains, so they were glad for Mrs. Dahlbe's berries, to make sauce and jam.

As they turned Birdie in the direction of home, Mama said thoughtfully, "If we were using an automobile and gasoline to do this, there wouldn't be much profit in it."

"That's right, Mama," Sarah agreed eagerly.

They reached the end of their lane and Mama was just going to turn the buggy into it, when she peered down another lane which cut across their own, at the highway. "I wonder . . ." she said. She pulled on Birdie's reins to bring her to a stop and sat, thinking and looking off down the other lane, which led to a horrible little house and a yard full of trash. An old man and woman, named Segner, lived there, with a big dog that barked all the time and a grownup daughter called Crazy Ellen. The Segners could speak only Norwegian. Sarah had been sent there once on an errand and she hoped she would never have to go again.

"The Segners don't have money to buy strawberries, Mama," Sarah said. She didn't want her mother to drive through the Segner lane, which was muddy, and she especially didn't want to have to go into that awful yard, where the dog was.

"I know. But those old folks like strawberries as well as you do, I expect, even if they can't pay for them. We'll still have two boxes left for supper if I take a couple to them before we go home." Mama headed Birdie down the choked, sopping, narrow road.

They hadn't gone far when the buggy wheels began to sink. Birdile, urged by Mama, struggled to pull the wheels free of the deep, sucking mud, but she couldn't.

66

Each time the horse pulled, her hoofs made the ground slipperier, and the wheels sank ever farther.

"It's no use," Sarah's mother said, finally. She got out of the buggy and walked through the mud and grass, carefully picking her way, to the horse's head. "We'll have to unhitch her and have Papa come back with one of the grays to pull the buggy out. You ride Birdie home, Sarah, and tell him—you may have to ride out to the field to find him. I'll go on over to the Segners on foot, with the berries, and visit with them while I wait for Papa."

"Oh, Mama! You ride Birdie home. I'll walk." Sarah didn't want to leave her mother there. "We can take berries to the Segners some other time."

Her mother continued to unhitch the horse. "Do as you're told," she said mildly, but in a voice that warned Sarah to stop arguing. When the horse was unhitched, Mama boosted Sarah onto Birdie's back, threw her the reins and told her to take her time.

Sarah, sending Birdie on a mild gallop up their own lane, thought tearfully that now Papa would for sure say that Birdie was not worth her feed, getting stuck in the mud like that. As if a Ford wouldn't get stuck even worse, in an awful lane like the Segners', she thought. But she probably wouldn't dare say that to Papa.

7 *chapter*

Katie's mother married bachelor Andrew Sorenson in early June. They stood up together in the Dahlbe parlor, with Sarah's mother and father for witnesses and with Pastor Lindgren reading the marriage service over them. While the bride and groom were away on a week's honeymoon, Katie was going to stay with the Dahlbes, and Sarah and Katie could hardly wait for the wedding to be over, when it would be time for their visit together to begin.

As Pastor Lindgren was going out the door with

his wife, after the wedding, and after Katie's mother and her new husband had driven off in Andy Sorenson's car, the minister turned to the two little girls. "Mrs. Lindgren says that you haven't stopped in to see our baby for a long time," he said. "Did you know he has two teeth now?"

The girls shook their heads. They loved to go over to the minister's house during noon hours at school, after they had eaten their sandwiches, and watch the baby have his bath, but Mama had said that Mrs. Lindgren had enough to do without being bothered with them. "I don't like the children to make a nuisance of themselves," she said now to the pastor's wife. "I told Sarah not to go any more unless she was invited."

"Oh, now, Mrs. Dahlbe," Mrs. Lindgren protested. She was young and pretty, with soft yellow hair, and black eyelashes framing her hazel eyes. "Sarah and Katie are always welcome at my house. They're never any trouble."

"Well, if you want them—" said Mama.

"I do, I really do," the pastor's wife said.

After the Lindgrens left, Sarah's mother changed into old clothes and went out to help Papa with the chores. The two girls were left to do the dishes by themselves.

"I don't mind doing dishes when there's someone to talk to, do you, Katie?" Sarah asked.

"I always mind doing dishes!" Katie went over to the table and began taking crumbs from the plate on which there were several wedges left from the bridal cake. "I've got a stepfather," she said suddenly, trying to sound boastful. But Sarah heard the catch in her friend's voice. She said quickly, "Let's each wrap a piece of cake in a napkin, to put under our pillows, Katie. Mama says if you sleep on a piece of wedding cake, and make a wish, it's bound to come true."

Katie turned around, her eyes bright. "I'm going to wish for new slippers."

Later, after the girls were in bed, Sarah's mother came upstairs to their room. She said she was going to pretend that both Sarah and Katie were her little girls, while Katie's mother was away. She heard their prayers and tucked the covers around both of them, kissing each one good night.

"You can talk for half an hour, and then I want you both to settle down to sleep," she said. "You'll have a whole week together, you know."

"We can't go to sleep right away!" Sarah protested, but after her mother had gone, Katie fell asleep right in the middle of a story Sarah was telling her. Sarah took one last look through the window at the moon hanging from a branch of one of the cottonwood trees, and went to sleep herself.

The week of Katie's visit seemed to whizz by. One day the two girls and Hilmer helped Mr. Dahlbe in the potato field. Potato bugs were eating the plants; Sarah's father dusted them with some powder and then the children came along and knocked the dead and half-dead insects into pails. After all the bugs had been collected, Mr. Dahlbe dumped them out of the pails, into a heap, and burned them.

"That's the worst I've ever seen the potato bugs," Papa said. "Must be all the rain we had. We wouldn't have had a potato even for ourselves this winter, if we hadn't got rid of those bugs."

"Can Katie and I go and play now, Papa?" Sarah asked. There always seemed to be extra work in the summer time. Sometimes it was pulling weeds—although, by the end of June, the crops were too well along for much weeding. Picking up the windfall apples in the orchard was another summer job. The Duchess and Harvest apples were the first to ripen, and then came the Wealthies and the winter apples.

Mama also sent the two girls into the haybarn and chicken house, to gather eggs. Some of the hens tried to hide them, and one old hen kept laying eggs right in the feed box of one of the cow stalls.

The girls didn't work all the time. They spent hours playing in the woods or the orchard, with their dolls, or making miniature farms using twigs for fences and leaves for houses and barns, in the soft dirt. Nearly every afternoon while Katie was there, Sarah got permission to ride Birdie out to the rock pile, with Katie behind clinging to Sarah's waist.

On Friday night of the week of Katie's visit, the girls had an argument after supper and Mrs. Dahlbe ordered them outdoors. "Go and run off your orneriness," she told them. "I'll call you in when it's bedtime."

Sarah and Katie went outdoors, but they didn't play together. Sarah went over to the rain barrel under the downspout of the barn eaves, and began to float dandelion curls on the dark water, watching her friend out of the corner of her eye to see if Katie was going to join her. Katie, however, was sitting on the grass, pretending to look for four-leaf clovers, and ignoring Sarah. Sarah, not really enjoying playing with the dandelion curls all alone, was thinking of sauntering over, to start some kind of conversation so they could make up, when she saw a car coming up the lane.

"Somebody's coming!" she called.

Katie jumped to her feet. "It's Ma!" she yelled. "I bet it's Ma and Andy."

But it wasn't, it was Sarah's Uncle Adolf. He had brought a pony for Hilmer, in a two-wheeled cart he had hitched to the back of his car. "I always wanted a Shetland pony myself," he said, "so I traded one of my pigs for this one of Rassmussens'."

Hilmer stared from his uncle to the pony. "Is it mine, Uncle Adolf?" he asked. "All mine?" Hilmer's eyes were like blue diamonds in his brown face, as he walked toward the little dun-colored horse with white spots on its sides, and laid his face against the shaggy white mane.

"You shouldn't have done it, Ade!" Mama, who had come out of the house at Sarah's and Katie's shouts, shook her head at her brother-in-law.

"Ah!" Uncle Adolf wrinkled his nose at Mama. "Don't worry about the expense, Lena. I'll see to giving him his feed, at least the first year. Maybe the next year Hilmer will be big enough to work out the feed." He turned to Hilmer. "Why don't you get on him?" He gave Hilmer a boost onto the pony's back.

With envious eyes Katie watched Hilmer walk the pony around the yard. "Can I ride him once, when you've had your turn, Hilmer?" she asked.

"I'll have to get him broken in first," Hilmer said importantly, "before he'll let a girl get on him."

The grownups all laughed, but Sarah didn't.

"You spoil us, Ade," Mama said to Uncle Adolf, watching Hilmer with a soft look in her eyes.

"Who else have I got to spoil?" Uncle Adolf turned to Sarah's father. "I've had such good luck, every time I turned around this year, that I've ordered a new car. It has to be brought from Des Moines, though. Lund doesn't handle Overlands."

"An Overland!" Papa stared at his brother. "What do you want with such a big car?"

Uncle Adolf shrugged. "I don't know. Maybe the money I've made is just burning a hole."

With Uncle Adolf driving an Overland, Papa would be even more anxious to get a car of some kind, Sarah thought miserably. Nobody would care what happened to Birdie, now. Hilmer wouldn't think about anything except his pony, and if Papa got a car he would forget what a wonderful friend Birdie had been to him. She glanced at her mother. Probably even Mama wouldn't bother with Birdie after the baby came.

"Aren't you going to ride the pony, Sarah?" Mama asked, after Katie and Hilmer had both taken turns on the new little horse.

Sarah shook her head and looked at the ground so Mama wouldn't see how close she was to tears. "I don't want to," she said. As soon as she had a chance,

74

she wanted to go out to the barn and talk to Birdie. Birdie wasn't going to be very happy when the new pony was led into the barn with everybody making a fuss over it.

Suddenly Papa burst out, "I expect to be getting a car myself, this fall."

Sarah sucked in a breath to keep herself from crying out, "No, Papa! Don't buy a car." She stood silent, watching her parents' and her uncle's faces. After a minute, Mama said, "I guess that will take a little thinking over, Lars. We'll have to see how it goes with the corn. If we have an early frost—"

Uncle Adolf said, as if apologizing, "I didn't plan to stay. I promised Rassmussen to have this trailer of his back tonight." He re-fastened the gate on the cart and got into his car. "Good night, folks." To Hilmer he called, "Don't wear the pony out. There'll be plenty of time to ride him, you know." He drove off, sounding his automobile horn twice as he disappeared around the corner of the house.

"Adolf is one for surprises, all right," Mama said. She didn't look at Papa.

"Yah—it runs in the family." Papa didn't look at Mama, either, Sarah noticed. It was a little like her and Katie, she thought, when they'd had a quarrel. They really wanted to make up, but neither one knew just how to do it, or maybe they weren't sure they

76

wanted to. Except that there hadn't been any quarrel between Mama and Papa, that Sarah knew of.

"Maybe you'd better help Hilmer fix a stall for the pony, Lars." Mama's voice was calm as she turned toward the house. "The stars are beginning to show. It's time the youngsters were getting ready for bed."

"The pony can have the end stall. It's smaller than the others." Papa took a step toward Mama. "Lena . . ."

She turned and smiled at him, gently. "Never mind now, Lars. It's all right. We'll talk about it when the children are in bed."

Talk about what? Sarah wondered. The pony? Uncle Adolf? Getting a Ford? Maybe, she thought with hope, Papa and Mama were going to talk about Birdie, about a plan to buy an automobile but keep Birdie and the Shetland pony, too.

Nobody knew quite how it happened, but one morning when Mama was going to drive into town with the buggy, Papa went out to the pasture to catch Birdie and found her with a bad cut on her leg.

"It's that railroad fence," Papa said to Sarah's mother. "There's some loose barbed wire there. I've been aiming to fix it, but there's been so much else to do, I just haven't got around to it."

The whole family was in the barn. Papa had come in to fetch them after he found Birdie with the injury

78

and had led her into the barn. Mama brought out warm water and Papa washed the cut while Hilmer and Sarah watched and worried. Or anyway, Sarah worried. Hilmer had said he was going to be a veterinarian when he grew up and he seemed more interested than worried.

"You're welcome to that kind of work," Papa said. He didn't like to have to doctor anyone, not even a horse, but farmers had to look after their own animals, well or sick, unless they were rich and could hire the veterinarian to come out for every little trouble that came along.

"It's a bad cut." Sarah's father bent over Birdie's leg after he had cleaned it out and took a good look. "We'll have to talk to the doc about it, but maybe he won't have to come out. He charges pretty high for coming."

"Watch out, Lars!" Mama warned.

Sarah, thinking Mama meant that Birdie was going to kick, started to say that Birdie would never in a million years hurt anybody, when she saw that was not what her mother meant. Glancing at her father, Sarah saw that his face was pale under his deep tan and that as he stood up he swayed a little.

"I'm not going to keel over!" Papa answered sharply. But he put a hand on Sarah's shoulder, to steady himself.

79

Later, when Sarah and her mother were alone in the house, Mrs. Dahlbe explained that Papa couldn't stand any kind of sickness or accident. Especially not since the time Mr. Rusley had been gored by the bull. "It just seems like he wants to faint as soon as there's anyone hurt around him," Mama said. She and Sarah were cleaning the parlor. Mrs. Dahlbe had covered her head with a dust cap, and Sarah smiled at the way her mother looked, with loose hair coming out from under the cap, and her eyeglasses, as usual, halfway down her nose. Mama always cleaned house with such force that she came all apart.

"That's why," her mother went on, giving a long dangling cobweb a big sweep, "your father insists that I go to the hospital at Arden when the baby comes. He says he never wants to go through another time like Hilmer's being born. The midwife was late and it looked for a while like Papa was going to have to do it all alone."

"Do what, Mama?" Sarah wiped the little knobs that were pushed in and out when anyone played the organ. Her mother didn't answer so Sarah asked again, "Do what, Mama? What did Papa almost have to do by himself?"

"Never mind. I can't explain it now. All I meant to say was that I'll be going to the hospital to have this baby, although I don't see how we can afford it." Mrs.

Dahlbe sighed and, lowering her broom, wiped her forearm across her perspiring forehead. "Not if we're going to buy an automobile, too."

Sarah's hand stopped wiping the knobs. "Are we going to buy one, Mama?" She didn't really need to ask; she had seen it coming all summer long. And now that Birdie had a bad leg, it wasn't really any use hoping Papa would keep Birdie very long, now that she couldn't even pull the buggy. Uncle Adolf was sending his horse King over for them to use for a while; he never used a buggy any more, since he bought his Overland. He was coming at noon, and Sarah and her mother were hurrying to get through with the cleaning before then. Sonora Holten was having a birthday party in the afternoon and Sarah and Katie were both invited; Sarah even had a new dress of yellow organdy! It wasn't brand new, as she had hoped, but had come from her cousin in Dakota, the way so many of her dresses did. Still, Mama had starched the ruffles so they fluffed out as well as Katie's.

When Uncle Adolf arrived, he tied King to a post and went with Papa to take a look at Birdie's cut. Sarah waited anxiously to hear what her uncle would say about Birdie.

"The cut's in a bad place all right," was the verdict, given while Uncle Adolf was washing his hands at the kitchen sink. He dumped the basin of soiled water down the drain, pumped a clean one from the cistern to rinse the soap off, and took the towel Mama handed him. "Every time Birdie moves her leg, that cut's apt to break open. Maybe Doc Bruin could suggest something to do."

"Lena's going to stop in to see the vet when she goes into town this afternoon." Papa pulled his chair out and asked his brother to take the one next to him at the table in the dining room. "Come on, folks, let's eat while the food's hot. We'll worry about our Birdie, later."

Sarah, taking her own place at the table, remembered that Papa called Birdie "our Birdie" when he was thinking how much the horse meant to him. It was only when he thought about what an expense she was, and how old-fashioned it was to keep a horse and buggy, with everybody else driving cars, that he called Birdie "that nag" or "dumb critter"—expressions that hurt Sarah as much as if Papa had said them to her.

They were almost through eating when Papa said suddenly, "You really can't tell, though, what that horse might do. Remember, Lena, that time when Sarah was a baby, and our Birdie got the heaves?"

Sarah loved this story. She put down her biscuit to listen to Papa tell it. "That was one time I called the horse doc right away, because we couldn't get along without a horse for the buggy—it was before you came across from Norway, Ade. That poor horse was heaving so hard, it just about tore me to pieces, watching," Papa said. "The doc said it was hopeless; there wasn't much you could do for a horse with the heaves, but I covered her with blankets, and went out with a lantern to sit up all night in the barn with her."

Mama sniffed as though she wanted to cry at this

83

point. She said to Uncle Adolf, "Have some more potatoes. There's plenty." Then she said, "That was before we got the light plant, so there wasn't any light in the barn."

"Hilmer wasn't even born!" Sarah put in, to remind Papa how the story was supposed to go.

Her brother glared at her. "I was too!" he said.

Papa told them to stop arguing so he could finish his story.

"I was sitting out there on a pile of straw and thinking how long Birdie and I had known each other, and now she was dying. I'd have to get a new horse, that I knew, but there wasn't likely ever to be a horse like Birdie, for me." He tossed Mama a teasing look. "It was Birdie your ma really fell for, you know, Sarah. She was crazy for that horse, first time she got a look at her."

"Oh, you!" Mama said, but she didn't deny it.

"Anyway, I was out there alone with Birdie, feeling lower than a snake, when the barn door opened and who should come in but Lena. It was past midnight by then and she should have been in bed but she couldn't stand to think of me sitting up all night with a sick horse, especially our Birdie, and her not alongside of me. She said she'd come to take my place but I wouldn't let her do that. I went into the house and brought the baby in her cradle right out to the barn." He smiled at Sarah. "Guess who that baby was," he said.

"Me!" Every time she heard the story, Sarah wished she could remember back to being there in the barn with Mama and Papa. "Tell the end of the story now, Papa, please." The end was the best part.

"There wasn't much to it. When the sun came up in the morning, that crazy horse gave a snort or two, got up on her four legs, and when we took her by the halter she walked right outdoors, strong as you please. We had seen the heaves slow down sometime in the night, but we thought it meant she was dying, instead of getting well."

"It was a miracle," Mama said.

"Your miracle, Lena." Papa reached for a second soda biscuit, buttered it, and then dipped it in the syrup on his plate. "If you ever need nursing, Ade, you'd better send for Lena. She just don't let go, that woman."

When Sarah and her mother were driving to town behind Uncle Adolf's horse, Mrs. Dahlbe said, "Don't worry too much about our Birdie, Sarah. She's got a good constitution—I've a feeling in my bones about her. I think her cut will heal. But it's too bad it had to happen just now, when Papa has so much to worry about."

"Is Papa worried about the crops?" Grownups were always worrying about crops. They worried if it rained too much in the spring, or if it rained too little. They worried about the corn, especially. If there wasn't enough hot weather, it didn't ripen right and fill out the ears. They worried if frost came too early in the fall and they worried if it came too late. Corn had to freeze before it could be husked, but if a blizzard came early and filled the fields with snow, the men couldn't get into the fields to do the husking.

"Oh, I guess Papa's not so worried about crops—it's more me and the new baby. And Birdie's leg, if it shouldn't heal . . ." Mama sighed. "There's not much use fighting the times, I guess. We'll have to scrape up the money, somehow, for a car."

When Mama said it, then it was really going to happen. Sarah was quiet for the rest of the journey into town. Even the yellow ruffles on her dress, and the shiny patent leather of her shoes, gleaming from the vaseline she had rubbed into them, didn't seem as wonderful as they had been when she put them on.

When they picked up Katie she asked, "Have you got a new horse?" looking with surprise at King.

"This is my uncle's horse." Sarah explained about the cut on Birdie's leg. She added, "Birdie's sick."

"Is she going to die?" Katie asked.

"No!" Sarah almost wanted to slap her friend for

even asking such a thing. Birdie was not going to die—and she wasn't going to be sent away, either, no matter what Papa and Mama decided about buying a car. But way down deep she was not so sure and she went to the birthday party with a big worry right in the middle of her stomach.

Two weeks after Birdie's accident threshing day came. The evening before, Hilmer and Sarah were in the side yard when the threshing machine came up their lane. They ran to the front stoop to watch the steam engine pull the big thresher with its tall blower, into their yard. When the threshing rig and its crew came, even Sarah's town friends wished they lived in the country. It was exciting to help set the long tables for the ten or fifteen men from nearby farms who came to help, and it was fun to watch the thresher separate the heads of barley and oats from the dry stems which then became straw. When Papa let them, Hilmer and Sarah and Katie rode on top of one of the grain wagons on its trip from the threshing machine in the field to the granary just inside the windbreak trees.

After the thresher puffed around the corner of the Dahlbe drive and headed out to the west field, Sarah went into the house to tell her mother that Mr. Kramer had brought the threshing rig. All day long, Mama and Katie's mother—who had come up to help—

had cooked and baked and planned for the working crew the next day. Katie and her mother had gone home, but they would be back the next morning.

"Everything smells so good that I'd like to taste every single thing I see," Sarah said, eyeing the freshly frosted cakes, the bowls of raspberry sauce, the newly-baked bread.

"Well, you're not going to! I thought you and Katie and Hilmer would all have stomach aches, sure, the way you've been eating and tasting all day long. There's no need to act like a pig, Sarah. Gluttony is a sin."

Sarah felt tears sting her eyes. She knew her mother was tired—there were lavender shadows under Mama's eyes and she sat down twice as often as she usually did—but she didn't need to take her head off, all the same. Sarah went over to the window, blinking back the tears. Last year, on threshing day, she had ridden Birdie out to the fields to tell the men in the crew that it was time for lunch. This year, she or Hilmer would have to walk. And now Mama was cross and tired. It just seemed like the end of the world.

From behind her, Mama said, in a different voice, "Sarah, will you go and get my carpet slippers from the closet under the stairs? My feet are like boils."

"Oh, I'll be glad to, Mama!" Sarah went flying to the closet, felt around in the dimness for the carpet slippers, and hurried back to the kitchen with them. "Let me unlace your shoes for you, Mama," she said. Sarah sat down on the floor by her mother's feet, and her mother put a hand on her daughter's head for a minute. When the slippers were on, and Sarah was standing up again, she asked, "When is Papa coming in?"

"Not for quite awhile. He's got a lot of chores; they're going to start threshing at seven tomorrow, so they'll finish early," Mama said. "I told him to send Hilmer in; you children must get to bed. Tomorrow will be a hard day for all of us."

She wouldn't have a chance to ask her father how Birdie's cut was, tonight, Sarah decided. There was no use asking Hilmer; he didn't yet understand any more about cuts than she did.

Early next morning, Sarah caught her father just as he came out of the cow barn with a pail of milk. "Papa," she asked breathlessly, "is Birdie any better?"

With his free hand he pulled one of Sarah's braids, gently. "That horse is crazy. I went in to have a look at that leg of hers this morning, before I milked the cows, and it's plain as the nose on your face—" Papa let go of Sarah's braid and pinched her nose, instead, "—that Birdie's been saving that leg. The cut's healing. If the leg hasn't stiffened up too much, our Birdie's apt to be as good as new. Looks like I won't have to shoot her, after all."

"Papa!" Sarah wasn't really as shocked as she sounded; she knew when her father was teasing. She pulled away from him and went running toward the horse barn, to see for herself how Birdie was. She didn't know much about bad cuts, but she knew Birdie.

When Sarah reached her, Birdie whinnied, turned her head and looked right at Sarah. Sarah put an arm up over the horse's neck and stroked the brown, sleek hair with her other hand.

"You're going to get well, Birdie!" she said joyfully. "You're going to be good as new. Papa said so—and I say so, too." It hadn't done any harm, she thought, to put Birdie into her prayers every night.

9 *chapter*

School started again the first week of September. Sarah and Katie were in fifth grade now, and they had a brand new teacher. Her name was Miss Rodgerson and she had dark, curly hair and pretty brown eyes. Both of the girls felt sure they were going to be crazy about her. On their way home, they talked as fast as their tongues would go, about the exciting new teacher, and the big, tough-looking new boy, and when they were going to buy their schoolbooks.

At Katie's house, Sarah sat down on the front steps

for a few minutes but she didn't go into the house because her mother had said for her to come right straight home after school.

"There's going to be a surprise waiting for you and Hilmer," Mama had said.

"You mean our new baby?" Sarah had asked, astonished. The baby wasn't supposed to be born until November.

"No, no." Mrs. Dahlbe had been braiding Sarah's hair. She wound a string around the ends of each braid and then looped them and tied a hair ribbon across the back to hold the braids together. "I'm not going to say what it is. It's a surprise, that's all."

Sarah, the braids finished, turned around to look into her mother's face. "A good surprise?" she asked. Because Mama didn't sound so terribly cheerful.

"A good surprise."

So now Sarah rested only a minute or two at Katie's and then sped toward home, her legs moving faster than usual.

The lane was dry and dusty and the grass in the ditches beside it was dust-covered, too. Sarah stopped to scratch at a mosquito bite on her right leg. Soon there wouldn't be any crickets singing in the meadow, and the corn leaves in the fields would rattle like paper. Fall was here and after that there would be winter.

Christmas. Mama said thinking about things too far ahead of time spoiled them.

Sarah hurried up the lane, feeling hot and tired but growing more and more excited the closer she came to the house. Maybe the surprise was company. Maybe her cousins from North Dakota had come for a visit.

She broke into a run as she reached the driveway

and started around the house. Hilmer, who got out of school a half-hour earlier than she did, was probably already home and would see the surprise first. She saw the surprise as soon as she rounded the corner and all the joy slid out of her. There in the yard was a brand new Ford, its black paint shining in the sun, a spare tire decorating the space behind the fender on the driver's side. Hilmer was standing on the running board. When he saw Sarah he blew the horn very loud.

"It's ours!" he yelled. "It's ours!"

Sarah came slowly toward the shiny vehicle. Her mother was standing in the kitchen doorway, watching, and her father was polishing the glass on the headlamps, his expression a mixture of worry and pleasure. "That right lamp don't seem very bright," he said. "Lund better not have sold me a car with a short in the lamp."

"Well, what do you think of it, Sarah?" her father asked as she approached the new possession and stood silently beside it.

Sarah shook her head, finding no words to express the mixture of feelings inside herself. Katie's stepfather had a brand new Ford, and Uncle Adolf had an Overland. The banker had a Cadillac. Almost all the people they knew had some kind of automobile. Sarah would have been thrilled over the Ford except for the fear

94

that leaped at her: how soon would Papa get rid of Birdie, now that he had an automobile to drive?

Sarah's mother called from the doorway, "Come here, Sarah," and Sarah, suddenly overcome, ran across the yard and buried her face in her mother's apron. She hadn't known she was going to cry, but the tears seemed to pour from her.

"Now, now, darling," her mother said. "Now, now."

Mama almost never called either Hilmer or Sarah by any endearment, and Sarah, hearing the rare word, cried harder than ever. It was comforting to be held by Mama's plump arms.

At supper, Sarah asked the burning question: "Will you give Birdie away now, Papa?"

He was cutting slices of cold roast pork. His sharp knife stopped midway of a slice and his dark eyebrows lifted. "Why, no," he said. "We'll keep Birdie around awhile, for sure. Until spring, anyway. Mama can't drive the car, although she's bound to learn, in time."

A breath of relief escaped from Sarah, blowing across her plate and out across the room toward the window, where she could see the barn. Out of the depths of her relief, she said, "Are you going to take us for a ride in the Ford after supper, Papa?"

"Not tonight. Tomorrow night, maybe. For one thing, I have to give Birdie her final dose of that salve, after we finish eating." He shook his head admiringly. "I tell you, that horse is a wonder. Everybody said she'd never heal that cut but there she is, eating enough for two horses."

After Sarah had wiped the supper dishes, she slipped out of the house to the barn. A light shone, so she knew her father was there.

She crept past the work horses and past Hilmer's pony—she gave the Shetland a few affectionate strokes because Hilmer loved it—to the stall where Birdie was. Papa was there. He had Birdie's hoof in his hand and was studying the place below a white spot on her leg, where the wire cut had left the raw sore only six weeks earlier. "Look, Sarah," he said, beckoning to her to come closer. "You can hardly see where she was hurt." He stroked the horse's slender leg and reaching up, patted Birdie's flank. "Good girl, Birdie. They don't make horses like you nowadays."

Sarah, crouching down beside her father, looked carefully at Birdie's leg. The horse doctor had come only one time; the rest of the doctoring had been done by Papa and Mama and her and Hilmer. They had all taken turns washing out the cut and rubbing salve on it, and talking to Birdie to keep her from getting impatient and running out into the pasture. Sarah said softly, "She's our horse, Papa. Our Birdie. I love her, don't you?"

Her father put the horse's leg gently back on the stable floor and looked around at her. "Sure, I love her—if it's right to love an animal." He got to his feet then, adding gruffly, "Come along now, girl, into the house. It must be late."

September went by without frost, which made things look good for the corn crop. Papa was counting on it to make the money he had borrowed from Mama's chicken fund, for the Ford. Sarah, walking home from school toward the end of the month, felt a coolness in the wind that hadn't been there earlier. In the stubble of the harvested grain fields, she saw flocks of blackbirds settle like soot, and then rise again, to fly off southward. The few bluebirds that were around had already gone south; she'd seen the last ones sometime toward the end of August, gathering in the poplar tree at the edge of the Larsons' farm.

Behind her, as she turned into her own lane, she heard the sound of a car, and looking back, saw it was Uncle Adolf. He brought his car to a halt beside her and said, "Can I give you a ride somewhere, young lady?"

Sarah, giggling, crossed the lane.

"I looked for you in town," her uncle said, "but I didn't see hide nor hair of you. Well, walking is good for you, your ma says, so I guess it's all right." He gave her a sidewise look. "How do you like the Ford, Sarah-girl?"

"It's all right." Actually, Sarah had become quite fond of the Ford. It was nice to ride to church in it on Sundays and watch Papa park it alongside all the other automobiles in front of the church, instead of his having to drive Birdie and the buggy clear around to the back, where there were hitching posts. And on Sunday afternoons, Papa took them for drives along the highway, chugging along as fast as anyone else. Except for looking after the animals, Papa never worked on Sundays; he considered it a sin.

"Mama says that Birdie didn't get stuck as easy as the Ford does," Sarah said, loyally. Every morning now, Sarah went out to talk to Birdie for a few minutes before she went to school. Sarah did it partly because she felt guilty over not hating the new car as much as she thought she ought to.

As Sarah stepped into her uncle's Overland, she remembered something. She said, "Mama says you've got a sweetheart now, Uncle Adolf? Have you?"

His face, already burned red-brown from summer outdoors, turned a little darker. But he laughed. "Ask me no questions, I'll tell you no lies," he said.

It turned out that Uncle Adolf did have a sweetheart, somebody named Julia Krogstad, from over in

Mapleton. Sarah's mother invited Julia over to Sunday dinner and all the Dahlbes thought Uncle Adolf had made a good choice, after they met her.

"We're not going to get married until spring," Julia told them. "My mother's been sick, and I want to stay home until she feels better."

When Uncle Adolf and his sweetheart had driven off, Mama said to Papa, "Ade's going to get himself a good wife. A girl who is thoughtful of her mother and father, is going to look after her husband and children, too, when the time comes."

After the excitement of the engagement had died down, the Dahlbes all settled in to wait for the new baby's arrival. It wasn't due until November, but Mama said she wouldn't mind if it happened to come just a little sooner.

"Let me husk the corn in the big field before you decide to make your trip to the hospital," Papa said. He was going to stay home alone while Mama was away having the baby. Sarah would stay with the Sorensons and Hilmer would stay in town with Pastor Lindgren and his wife.

Mr. Dahlbe was plowing up a hayfield out near the end of the farm one Saturday morning around the middle of October, Hilmer with him, when Sarah's mother called upstairs for her to come right down to the kitchen. "Leave the bedmaking," she said, her voice a little sharp. "Hurry, Sarah."

Wondering and scared, Sarah ran down the back stairs as fast as she could. Her mother was standing near the stove, leaning on the back of a chair. She looked queer. She said, "Sarah, take Birdie or the pony, whichever one you can get a bridle on quickest, and ride out to Papa. Tell him to come home. I think the baby's beginning."

"Yes, Mama, I'll hurry. I'll go like the wind."

Sarah slipped into her jacket and pulled a stocking cap down over her ears, against the cold wind. She ran to the barn, her breath caught in her throat.

It didn't take long to put a bridle on Birdie. She stood very still while Sarah climbed on her by standing on the manger's rim. "You know it's important, don't you, our Birdie?" Sarah said to the horse as she rode out the barn door, ducking her head.

Hilmer, who was playing on the slough bumps near where Papa was plowing, saw Sarah coming and ran toward the hayfield to tell his father.

"What is it?" Papa asked as soon as Sarah reached him.

Sarah gave him her mother's message.

Papa's face turned the color it had that day when he got sick over Birdie's leg cut, but he hung onto Birdie's neck for a minute, until he felt better.

"Take Hilmer back with you and I'll bring the team and plow—quick as I can. Did Mama call the doctor?"

"I don't know." Sarah turned Birdie around and her father boosted Hilmer up behind her. They galloped back to the house, and throwing Birdie's reins over a hitching post, Hilmer and Sarah rushed into the house.

"Papa asked if you had called the doctor," Sarah said breathlessly.

"I called him, but he's in Des Moines. He won't be back until late tonight, his wife said." There was a frown between Mama's eyes—she kept looking out the window for Papa.

A few minutes later Papa came hurrying in the back doorway, telling Hilmer to go out and hold the team.

"I'll go get the Ford warmed up," Mr. Dahlbe said. "Lena, you call the doc and see if you can get hold of Ade—though he's probably out in the fields somewhere. I want him to come and take care of the chores while I drive you to Arden."

Mama explained again that the doctor would be out of town until evening. "There's no use your warming up the Ford, either, Lars. I'm not driving twenty miles with pains like these. This baby's made up its mind to be born at home." She bent over the chair again, for a minute.

Sarah's father stared at her mother. "It can't be born here. Not without the doctor."

Sarah's mother put a hand on her husband's arm. "We'll get Gert Sorenson to come up right away. And then, when she's here to stay with me, you can go get Mrs. Wick, the midwife. She'll do as good as the doctor—I can't wait for him."

"I'll call the Sorensons right away." Papa went to the telephone and began cranking the little handle. He cranked so hard the handle almost came off and he hollered at the operator that he was in a big hurry, and if anyone was on the Sorensons' party line, to ask them to hang up. In a minute, he had Katie's mother on the line. She said she would come right away, but she would have to walk, because Andy was off somewhere with the car and she didn't know when he'd be home.

Papa asked her to hold on and turned around to tell Mama. "I'll have to go after her," he said.

"No, you won't." Mama gave him a firm look. "You're going to stay right here with me, Lars Dahlbe, until someone else shows up. Sarah, you take Birdie and ride down to the Sorensons'. Gert Sorenson can ride Birdie back here. You girls stay down there awhile, until we phone you. Hurry, now, Sarah, that's my good, big girl."

Papa, grumbling and looking worried, told Mrs. Sorenson the plan and hung up. He called Uncle Adolf, but didn't get any answer, and Mama said he should try again later. In the meantime, the work horses could stay harnessed; it wouldn't kill them. When Adolf came, he would see to them and keep Hilmer out of the way, if need be. The last thing Sarah heard as she went flying out the door was Mama saying to Papa, "Now, calm down, Lars. There must be a million babies born every day. It's nothing so terrible. Gertie will be here in plenty of time; you won't be alone, whatever happens."

Maybe, Sarah thought as she and Birdie went galloping down the lane and out onto the highway, women were braver than men about some things. Mama was scared of thunderstorms and mice and fire but Papa wasn't. On the other hand, he was scared of people and animals being sick on his hands.

Mrs. Sorenson was waiting when Sarah got there and the two girls helped her onto Birdie's back. "I haven't ridden horseback in a long time," she said nervously, "but I guess I can manage it. Katie, you keep trying to locate Andy and tell him what's happening." From Birdie's back, she looked down at them. "Be good, now. And don't worry, Sarah. Your mama will be fine."

Sarah hadn't had time to worry, yet, but she was beginning to. The afternoon seemed the longest one that Sarah had ever spent. They washed all the dirty dishes and brought fresh drinking water in, to surprise

Katie's mother when she came home. They got out Katie's dominos and played a few games, but Sarah lost all the games because she wasn't paying attention; she kept listening for the telephone to ring. Every once in awhile, Katie would go and try to reach her stepfather at one of the places her mother had said he expected to be. She finally located him at the creamery and gave him the news. He came right home, stopping just long enough to see if the girls were all right alone, before going to Sarah's house to see if Katie's mother needed anything.

"How long does it take a baby to be born, Papa Andy?" Katie asked, as he was going out the back door.

He stopped, thinking hard, but finally had to say that he didn't know. They heard him crank his car and drive off; after that, the waiting was harder than ever. When the telephone rang, they both jumped. Katie ran across the room to answer it while Sarah listened with a pounding heart.

It was one of the ladies from the church, wanting to talk to Katie's mother. Katie told her where her mother was, and why, and then hung up. "We'll just have to think of something special to do," she said to Sarah, "so we won't be so jumpy." She had no more than got the words out of her mouth when the telephone rang again.

"It's for you, Sarah," Katie said, adding, "It's your papa."

"You have a new brother, Sarah." Papa sounded very happy. "Eight and a half pounds! He's a husky one, I tell you. Mama's fine, too. She said to call you and tell you first of all."

Sarah began to cry, and couldn't talk.

"Now, now, girl, there's nothing to cry about," her father said. "Next time we'll make it a sister, for you."

She wasn't crying because the baby was a boy, Sarah thought, but it was no use trying to explain to Papa. She managed to stammer something about being glad Mama was all right, and about the new baby brother, and then Papa turned the telephone over to Katie's mother who wanted to speak to Katie. Sarah remembered, after she had left the telephone, that she hadn't asked Papa what color eyes the baby had, or what they were going to name him.

10 *chapter*

The baby was christened Lawrence William after Papa, whose name was Lars Wilhelm—Mama said they didn't want two of exactly the same name in the family and Lawrence was close to Lars. Uncle Adolf and Aunt Julia, as Sarah and Hilmer had been asked to call Uncle Adolf's fiancée, were the sponsors when the baby was baptized, in November. Sarah and Hilmer and Mama and Papa sat in one of the front pews in church during the baptism and Sarah was very proud of her new brother because he didn't cry, not even when Pastor Lindgren dipped a hand into the baptismal font and sprinkled the water over Lawrence William's head. He was a very good baby. Mama said it was because he was healthy and strong and knew how welcome he was in their family.

The rest of the fall seemed to whirl by, and early in December, Papa said, the way he did every year, "Now, I want everybody to write out a list of what they want for Christmas. I'm not saying you'll get what you want, but it never hurts to ask."

Sarah had plenty of ideas to put down, but couldn't seem to get started.

Hilmer, across the table from her, was filling his sheet of paper fast, even though he couldn't write very well, yet. It was after supper. The oven door in the kitchen range was open and warmth poured through the doorway between the two rooms. In the sitting room, where the big heater was, Mama was folding clean clothes that had been drying in the spare bedroom, and Papa was frowning over something he was reading in the Cedar Grove paper.

Her father's frown made Sarah think of Birdie and what might happen to her, when spring came. After the baby had been born, Sarah had reminded her parents that if it hadn't been for Birdie, she wouldn't have been able to reach Papa in the field quickly, and Mrs. Sorenson wouldn't have been able to come to their house right away. Papa had admitted that Birdie had been a big help. "But I guess that was about the last sprint for the poor creature. She's been in the dumps ever since."

Sarah knew what Papa meant. When she went out to the barn every morning before school, she felt bad about how little sparkle Birdie had. But that was because Birdie never liked winter, Sarah told herself. In the spring, when the birds began to come again, and there was grass in the pasture instead of snow, Birdie would be like she had always been, other springs. Lively, bright-eyed, and ready to carry Sarah to the ends of the farm.

Sarah suddenly had an idea. She began to write slowly, "All I want for Christmas is our Birdie. I want her to be our horse forever and ever. Sarah." She folded the note carefully and put it in the cup where Papa had told her and Hilmer and Mama to put their Christmas wishes. Maybe it was too big a wish ever to come true but Papa had said that it never hurt to ask. She went into the sitting room, and bent over the baby who was lying on the couch wrapped in blankets, to give him a kiss on his soft cheek. She said, "I'm going to bed now, Mama." She didn't want to be around when Papa opened her Christmas list.

Christmas had three important parts to it. First there was the school program, second, Christmas Eve at home, and third, the program at the church on Christmas Night. The best part, to Sarah, was Christmas Eve.

"John Larson believes in Santa Claus," Hilmer said to Sarah on the morning of Christmas Eve. Mama had put Sarah's hair up on rags, for the morning services and the church program, which were the next day.

"Oh, John Larson!" Sarah was scornful. Mama said Christmas was the birthday of Jesus Christ and it was not right to celebrate such a holy day by pretending there was anyone like Santa Claus. Long ago, Mama had explained to Sarah, "Your Christmas presents come from Papa and me, and Uncle Adolf and Grandpa and other people, with God's blessing. The reason we celebrate Christmas is because a long time ago, in Nazareth, the Son of God was born. I want you always to remember that."

Sometimes, when Sarah felt a little unhappy because some of her friends believed in Santa Claus and it seemed to be fun, she made herself think hard about Jesus and his birthday. After all, she wouldn't want *her* birthday changed into some other kind of celebration, so why should the baby Jesus? Jesus, Pastor Lindgren told them in Sunday school, was still alive today, in spirit, so he would know about his birthday.

Christmas Eve day was always a long one and that year seemed worse than ever. But finally, Sarah and

Hilmer and Mama and Papa sat down to Christmas Eve supper of rice and raisin pudding and oyster stew, with *lutefisk* for Papa. Sarah usually ate two bowls of the stew but this night she couldn't, because of her special Christmas wish. Usually, Papa teased her and Hilmer about what they wrote on the slips of paper, but this year he had never once mentioned Sarah's wish to her. Mama hadn't, either, and Sarah was beginning to think she shouldn't have asked for something that was perhaps impossible to have. Papa would not send Birdie away unless he had to, but he might have to, and her putting it down as a Christmas wish would only make him feel worse, if he did.

After supper, Papa went out to finish the chores, and Mama, Sarah, and Hilmer washed and wiped the supper dishes. When Mr. Dahlbe came back inside, he went into the sitting room and lit the candles on the tree.

"Everybody ready?" he called out.

Mama went into the sitting room first, and then Sarah and Hilmer. The baby's crib was brought into the sitting room, so he could see the tree, too.

"It's beautiful," Sarah said in a whisper, staring at the fat, round tree Papa had placed in front of the glass doors which led to the parlor. They didn't keep the parlor open during the cold months; you could only see into it through the glass doors. The red and green candles reflected their flames in the glass, and threw light across the strings of popcorn, the cranberry ropes and the tinsel decorating the tree. At the last minute, Mama tied on the shining Christmas balls of silver and gold and red and blue and green. Then Papa reached up to the top and fastened the tinsel star on the tip of the tree.

Sarah turned to her mother. "Every year our tree looks more beautiful," she said.

"I think so, too," her mother agreed.

They sang carols then and Papa read the Christmas story from the Gospel according to St. Luke, and asked a blessing on his household, in the name of Jesus.

At last it was time to start handing out the presents that were under the tree. Uncle Adolf had come the night before with packages from him and Aunt Julia.

Sarah's first package turned out to be the gold bracelet she hadn't put on her list. "From Uncle Ade and Aunt Julia," it said.

"They must have guessed!" Sarah cried.

Her mother smiled. "Or a little bird told them." She got a brand new dress of brown wool, with gold-colored collar and cuffs of satin. Mama had made it, out of new material.

Hilmer, who had asked for a dozen things, got at

least two of them: a pair of ice skates and a new jacket.

Papa was almost at the end of the pile of presents. Sarah, thinking about her wish for Birdie, realized that it had been very silly. Birdie couldn't be wrapped up and put under a tree! Papa and Mama hadn't paid any attention to Sarah's foolishness; they had chosen what they thought she needed or wanted.

At last every package was gone from under the tree.

"*Gladlig Jule*," Papa called. That was Merry Christmas in Norwegian. He put his hand into his pocket and brought out an envelope. "Will you look at that?" he asked, pretending to be surprised. "I must have forgotten something." He looked hard at the envelope. "This says it is for Miss Sarah Helena Dahlbe. Anybody here by that name?"

"Me, Papa!" Sarah jumped to her feet and ran to take the envelope. She couldn't imagine what in the world it was.

Tearing it open, she glanced inside. There was a sheet of paper with words on it. Pulling out the paper, she read, in her father's handwriting:

"This is a certificate of ownership. Birdie Dahlbe, known as 'Our Birdie,' is from this day forward the sole property of Sarah Helena

113

Dahlbe. Our Birdie will not be sold, or given away, or otherwise disposed of, without the full consent of the owner.

Signed, Lars and Helena Dahlbe."

"Merry Christmas to you, Sarah," Mama said when Sarah had finished reading the note out loud.

"Does it mean that Birdie's mine, forever and ever?" Sarah asked.

"Yours," Mama corrected gently, "as long as she lives."

"And that will be forever!" Sarah cried, although she knew it couldn't ever come true.

Snow began to fall in the night and kept on falling. There had been snowfalls earlier but this was a real winter storm. Uncle Adolf and Aunt Julia almost got stuck in the lane with the Overland, which was heavier than the Dahlbe Ford, when they came from church to have Christmas dinner with them. By afternoon, there were several inches of white flakes covering the whole wintry world.

"You'd better drive your car into the surrey shed, next to ours," Papa said to Uncle Adolf. "We'll be lucky to get into the church tonight if this keeps up."

"We could go in the bobsled," Mama said.

"No need to do that," Uncle Adolf and Papa said

together, but at five o'clock, when they looked out of the front window in the parlor, they were not so sure.

"It won't hurt to put the box on the runners, anyway," Papa said.

Sarah and Hilmer put on heavy wraps, and Sarah wound her scarf around her neck to go out and watch the men fit the box of the sleigh on the big sled runners. Papa kept muttering, "We could probably make it in the cars," but Sarah noticed that he kept looking at the sky, where the fleecy flakes were coming down even more thickly than before.

By seven o'clock there was no question of cars being able to get through the lane.

"I'd love to ride in the bobsled," Julia said. "Maybe

I'll have to stay all night with you people, though, if Ade can't get his car out. Would that be all right?"

"You couldn't be more welcome," Mama said. "Ade will have to go home some way, though, to take care of his animals, but he can come back the next day to get you and his car."

"And how am I going to get home?" Uncle Adolf asked. "You think I'm going to walk six miles in a snowstorm?"

"You can ride one of the grays," Papa said.

Sarah's mother looked over at her.

Sarah thought hard for a minute.

She said, "You can take my Birdie, Uncle Adolf."

"*Your* Birdie?" Her uncle's eyebrows rose in the air.

Sarah told him about her Christmas present from Mama and Papa. When she had finished, her uncle laughed so hard she thought the plates would fall out of the cupboard. Then he said soberly, "Thank you very much, Miss Sarah, for offering to loan me your horse."

Usually, Uncle Adolf said, "*Mange tak*" and not "Thank you" and he had never before called Sarah "Miss." She felt a rich new sense of pride and ownership.

Thank you, she said under her breath as she stared at the blurred Christmas tree. She wasn't sure who she was thanking; she just knew that her heart was so full of love and happiness that she had to thank someone. Thank you for giving me Birdie forever and ever. Amen.

In the morning, before anyone else was up, she would plow her way through the snow to the barn and give Birdie her Christmas present: a crisp, winter apple from the cellar, cut into pieces just the right size for an old horse to eat.